ADVENTURE CLASSICS FOR BOYS

ROBINSON CRUSOE
TREASURE ISLAND
KIDNAPPED

Retold and abridged for
younger readers

EGMONT

EGMONT

We bring stories to life

Adventure Classics for Boys
First published in Great Britain 1963
as Famous Adventure Classics
by Golden Pleasure Books
This edition published 2011
by Egmont UK Limited
239 Kensington High Street
London W8 6SA

ISBN 978 1 4052 5465 6

1 3 5 7 9 10 8 6 4 2

A CIP catalogue record for this title is available from the British Library

Printed and bound in Spain

MIX
Paper
FSC FSC® C018306

Egmont is passionate about helping to preserve the world's remaining ancient forests. We only use paper from legal and sustainable forest sources, so we know where every single tree comes from that goes into every paper that makes up every book.

This book is made from paper certified by the Forestry Stewardship Council (FSC), an organisation dedicated to promoting responsible management of forest resources. For more information on the FSC, please visit **www.fsc.org**. To learn more about Egmont's sustainable paper policy, please visit **www.egmont.co.uk/ethical**.

The Life and
Surprising Adventures of

ROBINSON CRUSOE

of York, Mariner

by Daniel Defoe

I was born in the year 1632 in the city of York, of a good family, though not an English one, my father being a foreigner of Bremen, who settled first at Hull. He became quite rich as a merchant and, leaving off his trade, lived afterwards at York, from whence he had married my mother, whose relations were named Robinson, and from whom I was called Robinson Kreutznaer. But, by the casual corruption of words in England, we are now called, nay, we call ourselves, and write our name Crusoe, and so my companions always called me.

I had two elder brothers, one of whom was lieutenant-colonel to an English regiment of foot in Flanders, formerly commanded by the famous Colonel Lockhart, and was killed at the battle near Dunkirk against the Spaniards. What became of my second brother I never knew, any more than my father or mother did know what was to become of me.

Being the third son of the family, and not bred to any trade, my head began to be filled very early with rambling thoughts. I would be satisfied with nothing but going to sea, and my inclination to this led me so strongly against the will, nay, the commands of my father, and against all the entreaties and persuasions of my mother and other friends, that there seemed to be something fatal in my nature tending directly to the life of misery which was to befall me.

Being one day at Hull, I found one of my companions was going to London in his father's ship. I consulted neither Father nor Mother about the decision I had made, nor sent them word of it. Leaving them to hear of it as they might, and in an ill hour, God knows, on the 1st of September, 1651, I went on board a ship bound for London. Never any young adventurer's misfortunes, I believe, began sooner, or continued longer than mine. The ship was no sooner gotten out of the Humber but the wind began to blow, and the waves to rise in a most frightful manner. As I had never been at sea before, I was most inexpressibly sick in body, and terrified in my mind.

The sixth day of our being at sea we came into Yarmouth road. The wind having been contrary and the weather calm, we had made but little way since the storm. Here we were obliged to come to an anchor, and here we lay, the wind continuing contrary—namely, at south-west—for seven or eight days, during which time a great many ships from Newcastle came into the same roads.

We should not have ridden here so long, but have tided it up the river, except that the wind blew too fresh. And after we had lain four or five days, it blew very hard. However, the roads being reckoned as good as a harbour, and the anchorage good, our men were unconcerned, and not in the least apprehensive of danger, but spent the time in rest and mirth, after the manner of sailors. But the eighth day, in the morning the wind increased, and we had all hands at work to strike our topmasts, and make everything snug and close, that the ship might ride as easy as possible. By noon the sea went very high indeed, and we thought once or twice our anchor had come adrift, upon which our master ordered out the sheet-anchor, so that we rode with two anchors ahead, and the cables veered out completely.

By this time it blew a terrible storm indeed, and now I began to see terror and amazement in the faces even of the seamen themselves. The master, though vigilant in the business of preserving the ship, yet as he went in and out of his cabin by me, I could hear him softly to himself say several times, 'Lord be merciful to us, we shall be all lost, we shall be all undone;' and the like. During these first hurries I was stupid, lying still in my cabin, which was in the steerage, and cannot describe how I felt. I could ill reassume the first penitence, which I had so hardened myself against. I thought the bitterness of death had been past, and that this would be nothing, too, like the first. But when the master himself came to me, as I said just now, and said we should all be lost, I was dreadfully frighted. I got up out of my cabin and looked out, but such a dismal sight I never saw. The sea went mountains high, and broke upon us every three or four minutes. When I could look about, I could see nothing but distress round us. Two ships that rode near us we found had cut away their masts, being heavily laden, and our men cried out that a ship which rode about a mile ahead of us was foundered. Two more ships, being driven from their anchors, were run out of the roads to sea to possible wreck, and that with not a mast standing. The light ships fared the best, as not so much labouring in the sea, but two or three of them drove, and came close by us, running away with only their sprit-sail out before the wind.

Towards evening the mate and boatswain begged the master to let them cut away the foremast, which he was very unwilling to, but the boatswain protesting to him that if he did not the ship would founder, he consented. When they had cut away the foremast, the mainmast stood so loose, and shook the ship so much, they were obliged to cut her away also, and make a clear deck.

Anyone may judge the condition I was in at all this, who was but a young sailor, and who had been in such a fright before at but a little. But if I can express at this distance the thoughts I had about me at that time, I was in tenfold more horror of mind on account of my former convictions, and the having returned from them to the resolutions I had wickedly taken at first, than I was at death itself. And these, added to the terror of the storm, put me into such a condition that I can by no words describe it. But the worst was not come yet. The storm continued with such fury, that the seamen themselves acknowledged they had never known a worse. We had a good ship, but she was deep laden and wallowed in the sea, that the seamen every now and then cried out she would founder. It was my advantage in one respect that I did not know what they meant by founder till I inquired. However, the storm was so violent, that I saw what is not often seen —the master, the boatswain, and some others more sensible than the rest, at their prayers, and expecting every moment when the ship would go to the bottom. In the middle of the night, and under all the rest of our distress, one of the men that had been down on purpose to see, cried out we had sprung a leak. Another said there was four foot of water in the hold.

Then all hands were called to the pump. At that very word my heart, as I thought, died within me, and I fell backwards upon the side of my bed where I sat, into the cabin. However, the men roused me, and told me that I, that was able to do nothing before, was as well able to pump as another, at which I stirred up and went to the pump, and worked very heartily. While this was doing, the master, seeing some light colliers who, not able to ride out the storm, were obliged to slip and run away to sea, and would come near us, ordered to fire a gun as a signal of distress. I, who knew nothing what that meant, was so surprised that I thought the ship had broke, or some dreadful thing had happened. In a word, I was so surprised that I fell down in a swoon. As this was a time when everybody had his own life to think of, nobody minded me, or what was become of me; but another man stepped up to the pump, and thrusting me aside with his foot, let me lie, thinking I had been dead. It was a great while before I came to myself.

We worked on, but the water increasing in the hold, it was apparent that the ship would founder, and though the storm began to abate a little, yet as it was not possible she could swim till we might run into a port, so the master continued firing guns for help; and a light ship, who had rid it out just ahead of us, ventured a boat out to help us. It was with the utmost hazard the boat came near us, but it was impossible for us to get on board, or for the boat to lie near the ship's side. Then at last, the men rowing very heartily, and venturing their lives to save ours, our men cast them a rope over the stern with a buoy to it, and then veered it out a great length, which they after great labour and hazard took hold of, and we hauled them close under our stern, and got all into their boat. It was to no purpose for them or us after we were in the boat to think of reaching their own ship, so all agreed to let her drive, and only to pull her in towards shore as much as we could. Our master promised them that if the boat was staved upon shore he would make it good to their master, so partly rowing and partly driving, our boat went away to the norward, sloping towards the shore almost as far as Winterton Ness.

We were not much more than a quarter of an hour out of our ship when we saw her sink, and then I understood for the first time what was meant by a ship foundering in the sea. I must acknowledge I had hardly eyes to look up when the seamen told me she was sinking, for from that moment they rather put me into the boat than that I might be said to go in. My heart was, as it were, dead within me, partly with fright, partly with horror of mind and the thoughts of what was yet before me.

While we were in this condition, the men yet labouring at the oar to bring the boat near the shore, we could see, when, our boat mounting the waves, we were able to see the shore, a great many people running along the shore to assist us when we should come near. But we made but slow way towards the shore, nor were we able to reach the beach, till, being past the lighthouse at Winterton, the land falls off to the westward towards Cromer, and so the shore broke off a little the violence of the wind. Here we got in, and though not without much difficulty, got all safe on land, and walked afterwards on foot to Yarmouth, where, as unfortunate men, we were used with great humanity, as well by the magistrates of the town, who assigned us good quarters, as by particular merchants and owners of ships, and had money given us sufficient to carry us either to London or back to Hull, as we thought fit.

* * * * *

Had I now had the sense to have gone back to Hull, and have gone home, I had been happy, and my father, an emblem of our blessed Saviour's parable, had even killed the fatted calf for me. For, hearing the ship I went away in was cast away in Yarmouth road, it was a great while before he had any assurance that I was not drowned.

But my ill fate pushed me on now with an obstinacy that nothing could resist. I made voyage after voyage with varying luck, the last and most fatal on the same day of the month eight years past that I first left home.

We were bound from Brazil to the Guinea coast and had very good weather, only excessively hot, all the way upon our own coast, till we came just level with Cape St Augustino. From there, keeping farther off at sea, we lost sight of land, and steered as if we were bound for the Isle Fernand de Noronha, holding our course north-east by north, and leaving those isles on the east. On this course we passed the line in about twelve days' time, and were by our last observation in 7 degrees 22 minutes northern latitude, when a violent

[11]

tornado or hurricane took us completely by surprise. It began from the south-east, came about to the north-west, and then settled into the north-east, from whence it blew in such a terrible manner that for twelve days together we could do nothing but drive, and, scudding away before it, let it carry us whither ever fate and the fury of the winds directed. And during these twelve days I need not say that I expected every day to be swallowed up. Nor, indeed, did any in the ship expect to save their lives.

In this distress, the wind still blowing very hard, one of our men early in the morning cried out 'Land!' and we had no sooner run out of the cabin to look out in hopes of seeing whereabouts in the world we were, but the ship struck upon a sandbank. In a moment, her motion being so stopped, the sea broke over her in such a manner, that we expected we should all have perished immediately.

It is not easy for anyone who has not been in the like condition to describe or conceive the consternation of men in such circumstances. We knew nothing of where we were, or upon what land it was we were driven. As the rage of the wind was still great, we could not so much as hope to have the ship hold many minutes without breaking in pieces.

In this distress the mate of our vessel lays hold of the boat, and with the help of the rest of the men we got her slung over the ship's side, and getting all into her, let go, and committed ourselves, being eleven in number, to God's mercy and the wild sea.

After we had rowed, or rather driven, about a league and a half, as we reckoned it, a raging wave, mountain-like, came rolling astern of us, and plainly bade us expect the *coup-de-*

They got her slung over the ship's side

grace. It took us with such a fury, that it overset the boat at once, and, separating us from the boat and one another, gave us no time even to say, O God, for we were all swallowed up in a moment.

Nothing can describe the confusion of thought which I felt when I sunk into the water. Though I swam very well, yet I could not raise my head above the waves to draw breath. Then a wave, having driven me or rather carried me a vast way on towards the shore, and having spent itself, went back, and left me upon the land almost dry, but half-dead with the water I took in. I had so much presence of mind as well as breath left that, seeing myself nearer the mainland than I expected, I got upon my feet, and endeavoured to make on towards the land as fast as I could before another wave should return and take me up again. But I soon found it was impossible to avoid it, for I saw the sea come after me as high as a great hill, and as furious as an enemy which I had no means or strength to contend with.

The wave buried me at once twenty or thirty feet deep in its own body, and I could feel myself carried with a mighty force and swiftness towards the shore a very great way. But I held my breath, and assisted myself to swim still forward with all my might. I was ready to burst with holding my breath, when, as I felt myself rising up, so to my immediate relief I found my head and hands shoot out above the surface of the water. Though it was not two seconds of time that I could keep myself so, yet it relieved me greatly, gave me breath and new courage. I was covered again with water a good while, but not so long but I held it out, and finding the water had spent itself and began to return, I struck forward against the return of the waves, and felt ground again with my feet. I stood still a few moments to recover breath till the water went from me, and then took to my heels and ran with what strength I had farther towards the beach.

I was now landed and safe on shore, and began to look up and thank God that my life was saved as it had been, when some minutes before scarce any room to hope remained. I walked about on the shore lifting up my hands, and my whole being, as I may say, wrapped up in the contemplation of my deliverance, reflecting upon all my comrades that were nou lost, and that there should not be one soul saved but myself. For I never saw any of them afterwards, or any sign of them,

[14]

I walked about on the shore lifting up my hands

except three of their hats, one cap, and two shoes that were
not a pair.

I began to look round me to see what kind of place I was in,
for I was wet, had no clothes to change into nor anything to
eat or drink to comfort me. Neither did I see any prospect
before me but that of perishing with hunger, or being devoured
by wild beasts. And that which was particularly afflicting to
me was that I had no weapon, either to hunt and kill any
creature for my sustenance, or to defend myself against any
other creature that might desire to kill me for theirs. I had
nothing about me but a knife, a tobacco pipe, and a little tobacco in a box. Night coming upon me, I began, with a heavy
heart, to consider what would be my lot if there were any

ravenous beasts in that country, seeing that at night they always come abroad for their prey.

All the remedy that presented itself to me at that time was to get up into a thick bushy tree like a fir, but thorny, which grew near me, and where I resolved to sit all night. I walked about a furlong from the shore to see if I could find any fresh water to drink, which I did, to my great joy. Having drunk and put a little tobacco in my mouth to prevent hunger, I went to the tree, and getting up into it, endeavoured to place myself so as that if I should sleep I might not fall. There I fell fast asleep, and slept as comfortably as, I believe, few could have done in my condition.

When I waked it was broad day, the weather clear, and the storm abated, so that the sea did not rage and swell as before. But what surprised me most was, that the ship had lifted off in the night from the sand where she lay with the swelling of the tide, and was driven up to within about a mile from the shore where I was, seeming to stand upright still.

A little after noon I found the sea very calm and the tide ebbed so far out that I could come within a quarter of a mile of the ship. And here I found a fresh renewing of my grief, for I saw plainly that if we had kept on board we would all have been safe—we would all have got safely on shore, and I had not been so miserable as to be left entirely destitute of all comfort and company as I now was. This forced tears from my eyes again, but as there was little relief in that, I resolved, if possible, to get to the ship. So I pulled off my clothes, for the weather was extremely hot, and took to the water. When I came to the ship, and by the help of a rope got up into the forecastle of the ship, she had a great deal of water in her hold,

I pulled off my clothes and took to the water

but she lay so on the side of a bank of hard sand, that her stern lay lifted up upon the bank. By this means all her quarter was free, and all that was in that part was dry, for you may be sure my first work was to search and to see what was spoiled and what was not. And first I found that all the ship's provisions were dry and untouched by the water, and being very well disposed to eat, I went to the bread-room and filled my pockets with biscuit, and ate it as I went about other things, for I had no time to lose. I also found some rum in the great cabin, of which I took a large dram, and which I had need enough of to raise my spirits for what was before me. Now I wanted nothing but a boat to furnish myself with many things which I foresaw would be very necessary to me.

[17]

My raft was strong enough to bear any reasonable weight

It was in vain to sit still and wish for what was not to be had, and this extremity roused my ingenuity. We had several spare yards, and two or three large spars of wood, and a spare topmast or two in the ship. I resolved to fall to work with these, and flung as many overboard as I could manage from their weight, tying every one with a rope that they might not drift away. When this was done, I went down the ship's side, and pulling them to me, I tied four of them fast together at both ends as well as I could, in the form of a raft, and laying two or three short pieces of plank upon them crossways, I found I could walk upon it very well.

My raft was strong enough to bear any reasonable weight. I first got three of the seamen's chests, which I had broken open and emptied, and lowered them down upon my raft. The first of these I filled with provisions—namely bread, rice, three Dutch cheeses, and a little remainder of European corn which had been laid by for some fowls which we brought to sea with us, but which had been killed. After long searching I found out the carpenter's chest. I got it down to my raft, complete as it was, without losing time to look into it, for I knew in general what it contained.

My next care was for some ammunition and arms. There were two very good fowling-pieces in the great cabin, and two pistols. These I secured first, with some powder-horns, and a small bag of shot, and two old rusty swords. I knew there were three barrels of powder in the ship, but knew not where our gunner had stored them. With much search I found them, two of them dry, though the third had taken in water. Those two I got to my raft with the arms, and now I thought myself pretty well freighted, and began to think how I should get to shore with them, having neither sail, nor rudder. The least capful of wind would have upset all my navigation.

For a mile or thereabouts my raft went very well, only that I found it drifted a little too far from the place where I had landed before. By this I perceived that there was some current in the water, and consequently I hoped to find some creek or river there, which I might make use of as a port to get to land with my cargo.

As I imagined, so it was. There appeared before me a little opening of the land, and I found a strong current of the tide set into it, so I guided my raft as well as I could to keep in the middle of the stream.

At length I spied a little cove on the right shore of the creek,

I set off, up to the top of the hill

to which with great pain and difficulty I guided my raft, and at last got near enough that, reaching ground with my oar, I could thrust her directly in.

My next work was to view the country, and seek a proper place for my home, where I could stow my goods. I took out one of the fowling-pieces and one of the pistols, and a horn of powder, and thus armed I set off on discovery up to the top of a hill, where I saw my fate to my great affliction—namely, that I was on an island surrounded every way with the sea. No land was to be seen, except some rocks which lay a great way off, and two small islands, nearer than this, which lay about three leagues to the west.

With this discovery, I came back to my raft, and fell to work to bring my cargo on shore, which took me the rest of that day. And what to do with myself at night I knew not. I was afraid to lie down on the ground, not knowing but some wild beast might devour me, though, as I afterwards found, there was really no need for these fears.

However, as well as I could, I barricaded myself with the chests and boards that I had brought on shore, and made a kind of hut for that night's lodging.

The next day I made another voyage and after this went every day on board, and brought away what I could get.

I had been now thirteen days on shore, and had been eleven times on board the ship, in which time I had brought away all that one pair of hands could well be supposed capable of bringing, though I believe verily, had the calm weather held, I should have brought away the whole ship piece by piece. But preparing the twelfth time to go on board, I found the wind begin to rise. It blew hard all that night, and in the morning when I looked out, behold, no more ship was to be seen!

* * * * *

I now banished any more thoughts of it, being now wholly employed about securing myself against either savages or wild beasts. I had many thoughts of the method for doing this, and what kind of dwelling to make, and whether I should make me a cave in the earth, or a tent upon the earth.

In search of a place proper for this, I found a little plain on the side of a rising hill, which rose up above it almost vertically as steep as a house-side, so that nothing could come down upon me from the top. On the side of this rock there was a hollow place worn a little way in like the entrance or door of a cave.

On the flat green, just before this hollow place, I resolved to pitch my tent.

Before I set up my tent, I drew a half-circle before the hollow place, which extended about ten yards from the rock, and twenty yards across at the rock face.

In this half-circle I pitched two rows of strong stakes, the longest end being out of the ground about five foot and a half, and sharpened on the top. The two rows did not stand above six inches from one another.

The entrance into this place I made to be, not by a door, but by a short ladder to go over the top. This ladder, when I was in, I lifted over after me. And so I was completely fenced in and fortified, as I thought, from all the world, and consequently slept secure in the night.

Into this fence or fortress, with infinite labour, I carried all my riches, all my provisions, ammunition, and stores. And I made me a large tent, which, to preserve me from the rains that in one part of the year are very violent there, I made double — namely, one smaller tent within, and one larger tent above it, and covered the uppermost with a large tarpaulin which I had saved from among the sails.

I went out once at least every day with my gun to see if I could kill anything for food, and to acquaint myself with what the island produced. The first time I went out I discovered that there were goats in the island—which was a great satisfaction to me, but they were so shy, and so swift, that it was the most difficult thing in the world to come at them. But I was not discouraged at this, not doubting but I might

The first shot I made killed a she-goat

now and then shoot one. It soon happened . The first shot I made I killed a she-goat which had a little kid by her which she gave suck to, which grieved me heartily. But when the old one fell the kid stood stock-still by her till I came and took her up. And not just this, but when I carried the old one with me upon my shoulders, the kid followed me right to my enclosure, upon which I laid down the dam and took the kid in my arms, and carried it over my fence, in hopes of bringing it up tame; but it would not eat, and so I was forced to kill it and eat it myself.

Having now brought my mind a little to relish my condition, and given over looking out to sea, to see if I could spy a ship,

I made me a table

I began to apply myself to make things as easy for myself as I could.

So I went to work. I had never handled a tool in my life, and yet in time, by labour, application, and contrivance, I found at last that I wanted nothing but I could have made it.

I made me a table and a chair in the first place, and this I did out of the short pieces of boards that I brought on my raft from the ship. And when I had wrought out some boards, I made large shelves of the breadth of a foot and a half one over another, all along one side of my cave. These were for tools, nails, and ironwork, and, in a word, to separate everything in their own places, so that I might come easily at them.

I knocked pieces into the wall of the rock to hang my guns and all things that would hang up.

So that had my cave been seen, it looked like a big general store of all necessary things, and I had everything so ready at my hand that it was a great pleasure to me to see all my goods in such order.

And now, in the managing of my household affairs, I found myself wanting in many things, which I thought at first were impossible for me to make, as indeed with some of them it was.

I was at a great loss for candles, so that as soon as ever it was dark, which was generally by seven o'clock, I was obliged to go to bed. The only remedy I had was, that when I had killed a goat I saved the tallow. And with a little dish made of clay, which I baked in the sun, to which I added a wick of some oakum, I made me a lamp and this gave me light, though not a clear, steady light, like a candle. In the middle of all my labours it happened that, rummaging my things, I found a little bag, which, as I hinted before, had been filled with corn for the feeding of poultry. What little remainder of corn had been in the bag was all devoured by the rats, and I saw nothing in the bag but husks and dust. Wanting the bag for some other use I shook the husks of corn out of it on one side of my fortification under the rock.

It was a little before the great rains that I threw away this stuff, taking no particular notice of it, and not so much as remembering that I had thrown anything there. Then, about a month after, or thereabout, I saw some few stalks of something green shooting out of the ground, which I fancied might be some plant I had not seen. I was surprised and perfectly asto-

The clusters of grapes were just now in their prime

nished when, after a longer time, I saw about ten or twelve ears come out which were perfect green barley, of the same kind as our European, nay, as our English barley.

I carefully saved the ears of this corn, you may be sure, in their season, which was about the end of June, and laying up every grain, I resolved to sow them all again, hoping in time to have a quantity sufficient to supply me with bread. But it was not till the fourth year that I could allow myself the least grain of this corn to eat, and even then but sparingly.

Besides this barley, there were about twenty or thirty stalks of rice, which I preserved with the same care, and whose use was of the same kind or to the same purpose—namely, to make

[26]

me bread, or rather food, for I found ways to cook it up without baking.

But to go back to my early days on the island.

I searched for the cassava root, which the Indians in all that climate make their bread of, but I could find none. I saw large plants of aloes, but did not then understand them. I saw several sugar canes, but wild, and, for want of cultivation, imperfect.

The next day, the 16th, I went up the same way again, and after going something farther than I had gone the day before, I found a brook, and the grasslands began to cease, and the country became more woody. In this part I found different fruits, and particularly I found melons and grapes. The vines had spread indeed over the trees, and the clusters of grapes were just now in their prime, very ripe and rich. This was a surprising discovery, and I was exceeding glad of them. I found an excellent use for these grapes, and that was to cure or dry them in the sun, and keep them as dried grapes or raisins are kept, which I thought would be, as indeed they were, wholesome and agreeable to eat, when no grapes might be to be had.

The 3rd of August I found the grapes I had hung up were perfectly dried, and indeed, were excellent good raisins, so I began to take them down from the trees. It was very happy that I did so, for the rains which followed would have spoiled them, and I had lost the best part of my winter food, for I had above two hundred large bunches of them. No sooner had I taken them all down, and carried most of them home to my cave, but it began to rain, and from hence, which was the 14th of August, it rained more or less every day till the middle

I diverted myself with talking to my parrot

of October, sometimes so violently that I could not stir out of my cave for several days.

Within doors—that is, when it rained, and I could not go out—I kept busy on the following tasks, always observing that all the while I was at work I diverted myself by talking to a parrot I had caught and teaching him to speak. And I quickly taught him to know his own name and at last to speak it out pretty loud—POLL, which was the first word I ever heard spoken in the island by any mouth but my own. This, therefore, was not my work, but an assistant to my work. Now, as I said, I had a great employment upon my hands, as follows — namely, I had long sought by some means or other to make myself some earthen vessels. I did not doubt but if I could find out any clay, I might botch up some such pot as might, being dried in the sun, be hard and strong enough. And as this was necessary in the preparing of corn, meal, &c., which was the thing I wanted, I resolved to make some as large as I could, and fit only to stand like jars to hold what should be put into them.

It would make the reader pity me, or rather laugh at me, to tell how many awkward ways I tried to make this paste; how many of them fell in, and how many fell out, the clay not being stiff enough to bear its own weight; how many cracked by the over-violent heat of the sun, being set out too hastily; and, in a word, how, after having laboured hard to find the clay, to dig it, to temper it, to bring it home and work it, I could not make above two large earthen ugly things—I cannot call them jars—in about two months' labour.

However, as the sun baked these two very dry and hard, I lifted them very gently up, and set them down again in two great wicker baskets which I had made on purpose for them, that they might not break. And as between the pot and the basket there was a little room to spare, I stuffed it full of the rice and barley straw. These two pots being always dry, I thought they would hold my dry corn, and perhaps the meal as well.

* * * * *

My clothes began to decay mightily. I could not go quite naked since I could not bear the heat of the sun so well when naked as with some clothes. Indeed, the very heat frequently blistered my skin. No more could I ever bring myself to go

After this I spent a great deal of time to make me an umbrella

out in the heat of the sun without a cap or a hat, the heat of the sun beating with such violence as it does in that place that it would give me the headache presently.

I began now to save the skins of all the creatures that I killed—I mean four-footed ones—and I had hung them up stretched out on sticks in the sun, by which means some of them were so dry and hard that they were fit for little, but others were very useful. The first thing I made of these was a great cap for my head, with the hair on the outside to shoot off the rain. I did, in fact make it so well, that after this I made me a suit of clothes wholly of these skins—that is to say, a waistcoat, and breeches open at the knees, and both loose, for they were rather wanting to keep me cool than to keep me warm. I must acknowledge that they were wretchedly made, for if I was a bad carpenter, I was a worse tailor. However, they were such as I made very good shift with. And when I was outside, if it happened to rain, the hair of my waistcoat and cap being outermost I was kept very dry.

After this I spent a great deal of time and pains to make me an umbrella. I had seen them made in the Brazils, where they are very useful in the great heat which is there and I felt the heat every jot as great here, and greater too, being nearer the equinox. Besides, as I was obliged to be out much, it was a most useful thing to me, as well for the rains as the heats. I took a world of pains at it, and was a great while before I could make anything likely to hold. Nay, after I thought I had hit the way, I spoiled two or three before I made one to my liking. The main difficulty I found was to make it to let down. I could make it to spread, but if it did not let down too and draw in, it was not portable for me any way but just over my head, which would not do.

However, at last, I made one to answer, and covered it with skins, the hair upwards, so that it cast off the rains like a penthouse, and kept off the sun so effectually that I could walk out in the hottest of the weather with greater advantage than I could before in the coolest. And when I had no need of it, could close it and carry it under my arm.

★ ★ ★ ★ ★

I began now to notice my powder getting low, and I began seriously to consider what I must do when I should have no more. That is to say, how I should do to kill any goat.

[31]

I had, in the third year of my being on the island, kept a young kid, and bred her up tame, and I was in hope of getting a he-goat, but I could not by any means bring it to pass, till my kid grew old. And I could never find in my heart to kill her, till she died at last of old age.

But being now in the eleventh year of my residence, and, as I have said, my ammunition growing low, I set myself to study some art to trap and snare the goats, to see whether I could not catch some of them alive.

So I dug several large pits in the earth, in places where I had observed the goats used to feed. Over these pits I placed hurdles of my own making too, with a great weight upon them. On these I put ears of barley, and dry rice. I set three traps in one night, and going the next morning I found in one of them a large old he-goat, and in one of the other, three kids—a male and two females.

It was a good while before they would feed, but throwing them some sweet corn, it tempted them, and they began to be tame. And now I found that if I expected to supply myself with goat-flesh when I had no powder or shot left, breeding some up tame was my only way. Then, perhaps, I might have them about my house like a flock of sheep.

But then it presently occurred to me that I must keep the tame from the wild, or else they would always run wild when they grew up. And the only way for this was to have some enclosed piece of ground, well-fenced either with hedge or paling, to keep them in so effectually, that those within might not break out, or those without break in. This was a great undertaking for one pair of hands. Yet, I saw there was an absolute necessity for doing it.

[32]

In about a year and a half I had a flock of about twelve goats

I resolved to enclose a piece of about one hundred and fifty yards in length, and one hundred yards in breadth, which would maintain as many as I should have in any reasonable time, and, if my flock increased, I could add more ground to my enclosure.

This answered my end. And in about a year and a half I had a flock of about twelve goats—kids and all; and in two years more, I had three-and-forty—besides several that I killed for my food. And after that I enclosed five several pieces of ground to feed them in, with pens to drive them into, to take them as I wanted, and gates out of one piece of ground into another.

But this is not all, for now I not only had goat's flesh to

feed on when I pleased, but milk too—a thing which, indeed, in my early days, I did not so much as think of, and which, when it came into my thoughts, was really an agreeable surprise. For now I set up my dairy, and had sometimes a gallon or two of milk in a day. And as Nature, who gives supplies of food to every creature, also dictates naturally how to make use of it, so I, that had never milked a cow, much less a goat, or seen butter or cheese made, very readily and handily, though after a great many essays and miscarriages, made me both butter and cheese at last, and never went short of it afterwards.

It would have made a Stoic smile to have seen me and my little family sit down to dinner. There was my majesty, the prince and lord of the whole island. I had the lives of all my subjects at my absolute command—I could hang, draw, give liberty, and take it away; and no rebels among all my subjects.

But had anyone in England been to meet such a man as I was, it must either have frightened them, or raised a great deal of laughter. And as I frequently stood still to look at myself, I could not but smile at the notion of my travelling through Yorkshire with such an equipage and in such a dress. Be pleased to take a sketch of my figure as follows.

I had a great high shapeless cap, made of a goat's skin, with a flap hanging down behind, as well to keep the sun from me as to shoot the rain off from running down my neck—nothing being so hurtful in these climates as rain under the clothes. I had a short jacket of goat-skin, the skirts coming down to about the middle of my thighs, and a pair of open-kneed breeches of the same. I had on a broad belt of goat-skin dried, which I drew together with two thongs of the same, instead of buckles. Instead of a sword and a dagger hung

I was exceedingly surprised with the print of a man's naked foot

a little saw and hatchet, one on one side, one on the other. At my back I carried my basket; on my shoulder my gun; and over my head a great clumsy, ugly goat-skin umbrella—but which, after all, was the most necessary thing I had about me, next to my gun. My beard I had to allow to grow till it was about a quarter of a yard long. As to moustaches or whiskers I will not say they were long enough to hang my hat upon them, but they were of a length and shape monstrous enough, and such as in England would have passed for frightful.

But all this is by-the-by. For as to my appearance, I had so few to observe me, that it was of no manner of consequence, so I say no more about it.

Sometimes I went on long trips of exploration, and once I was out five or six days.

On one of the days, about noon, I was exceedingly surprised with the print of a man's naked foot on the shore, which was very plain to be seen in the sand. I stood like one thunder-struck, or as if I had seen an apparition. I listened, I looked round me; I could hear nothing, nor see anything. I went up to a rising ground to look farther. I went up the shore and down the shore, but it was all one, I could see no other impression but that one. I went to it again to see if there were any more, and to observe if it might not be my fancy; but there was no room for that, for there it was exactly, the print of a foot, toes, heel and every part of a foot. How it came thither I knew not, nor could in the least imagine. But after innumerable fluttering thoughts, I came home to my fortification, not feeling, as we say, the ground I trod on, but terrified to the last degree, looking behind me at every two or three steps, mistaking every bush and tree, and fancying every stump at a distance to be a man.

When I came to my castle, for so I think I called it ever after this, I fled into it like one pursued. Never frighted hare fled for cover with more terror of mind than I to this retreat.

I slept none that night. The farther I was from the occasion of my fright the greater my apprehensions were, which is something contrary to the nature of such things, and especially to the usual practice of all creatures in fear. But I was so em-barrassed with my own frightful ideas of the thing, that I

One of them immediately fell, being knocked down with a club

formed nothing but dismal imaginations to myself, even though I was now a great way off it. Sometimes I fancied it must be the devil, and reason joined in with me upon this supposition. For how should any other thing in human shape come into the place? Where was the vessel that brought him? What marks were there of any other footsteps? And how was it possible a man should come there? But, then, to think that Satan should take human shape upon him in such a place, where there could be no manner of reason for it except to leave the print of his foot behind him, and that for uncertain purpose, too, for he could not be sure I should see it. As I lived right on the other side of the island, he would never have been so simple as to leave a mark in a place where it was ten thousand to one whether I should ever see it or not, and in the sand, too, which the first surge of the sea upon a high wind would have defaced entirely.

Abundance of such reasons as these assisted to argue me out of all apprehensions of its being the devil. And I presently concluded, then, that it must be some more dangerous creature —namely, that it must be some of the very fierce savages of the mainland, who had wandered out to sea in their canoes, and either driven by the currents, or by conttary winds, had made the island. They had been on shore, but were gone away again to sea, being as loath, perhaps, to have stayed in this desolate island as I would have been to have had them.

While these reflections were rolling upon my mind, I was very thankful in my thoughts that I was so lucky as not to be thereabouts at that time, or that they did not see my cave, by which they would have concluded that some inhabitants had been in the place, and perhaps have searched farther for me. Then the terrible thought racked my imagination that they had found my cave. If so, I should certainly have them come again in greater numbers and devour me, or if they should not find me, yet they would find my enclosure, destroy all my corn, carry away all my flock of tame goats, and I should perish for mere want.

About a year and half after I had entertained these notions, I was surprised one morning early with seeing no less than five canoes all on shore together on my side of the island, and the people who belonged to them all landed!

While I was thus looking on them, two miserable wretches were dragged from the boats, where it seems they had been lying, and were now brought out for the slaughter. One of

I knocked him down with the stock of my gun

them instantly fell, being knocked down, I suppose, with a club or wooden sword—for that was their way—and two or three others were at work immediately cutting him open for their cookery, while the other victim was left standing by himself till they should be ready for him. In that very moment this poor wretch, seeing himself a little at liberty, nature inspired him with hopes of life, and he started away from them, and ran with incredible swiftness along the sand directly towards me.

I was dreadfully frighted, that I must acknowledge, when I perceived him to run my way. However, I kept my station, and my spirits began to recover when I found that there were not more than three men that followed him. And still more

He laid his head upon the ground and set my foot upon his head

was I encouraged, when I found that he outstripped them exceedingly in running, so that if he could but hold it for half an hour, I saw easily he would fairly get away from them all.

There was between them and my castle the creek where I landed my cargoes out of the ship, and this I saw plainly he must swim over, or the poor wretch would be taken there. But he made nothing of it, though the tide was then up, but plunging in, swam through in about thirty strokes, landed and ran on with great swiftness. When the three pursuers came to the creek, I found that two of them could swim, but the third could not. Standing on the other side, he looked across, but went no farther, and soon after went softly back again, which, as it happened, was very well for him in the main.

I observed that the two who swam were yet more than twice as long swimming over the creek as the fellow was that fled from them. It came now very strongly into my thoughts, that now was my time to get me a servant, and perhaps a companion or assistant, and that I was called plainly by Providence to save this poor creature's life. I immediately ran down the ladder with all possible expedition, fetched my two guns, and getting up again with the same haste to the top of the hill, I posted myself in the way between the pursuers and the pursued. Hallooing aloud to him that fled, he, looking back, was at first perhaps as much frighted at me as at them, but I beckoned with my hand to him to come back. Meantime I slowly advanced towards the two that followed. Then rushing at once upon the foremost, I knocked him down with the stock of my gun. I was loath to fire, because I would not have the rest hear. Having knocked this fellow down, the other who pursued with him stopped, and I advanced towards him. But as I came nearer, I perceived that he had a bow and arrow, and was fitting it to shoot at me, so I was then necessitated to shoot at him first, which I did and killed him at the first shot. The poor savage who fled, but had stopped, though he saw both his enemies fallen, and killed, as he thought, yet was so frighted with the fire of my gun, that he stood stock-still, and neither came forward nor went backward, though he seemed rather inclined to retreat than to come on. I hallooed again to him, and made signs to come forward, which he understood, and came a little way, then stopped again, and then a little farther,

He was a comely, handsome fellow

and stopped again, and I could then perceive that he stood trembling. I smiled and beckoned to him to come still nearer. At length he came close to me, and then he kneeled down again, kissed the ground, and laid his head upon the ground, and taking me by the foot, set my foot upon his head. This, it seems, was in token of swearing to be my slave for ever. I took him up and made much of him, and encouraged him all I could.

But that which astonished him most, was to know how I had

killed the other Indian so far off. Pointing to him, he made signs to me to let him go and see, so I bade him go as well as I could. When he came to him he stood like one amazed, looking at him, turned him first on one side, then on the other, looked at the wound the bullet had made, which it seems was just in his breast, where it had made a hole, and no great quantity of blood had followed; but he had bled inwardly, for he was quite dead. My savage took up the man's bow and arrows and came back, so I turned to go away, and beckoned to him to follow me.

He was a comely, handsome fellow, perfectly well-made, with straight strong limbs, not too large, tall and well-shaped, and as I reckon, about twenty-six years of age. He had a very good countenance, not a fierce and surly aspect, and seemed to have something very manly in his face. His hair was long and black, not curled like wool; his forehead very high and large, and a great vivacity and sparkling sharpness in his eyes. In a little time I began to speak to him, and teach him to speak to me. And first, I made him know his name should be Friday, which was the day I saved his life. I called him so for the memory of the time. I likewise taught him to say Yes and No, and to know the meaning of them. I gave him some milk in an earthen pot, and let him see me drink it before him, and sop my bread in it. And I gave him a cake of bread to do the like, which he quickly complied with, and made signs that it was very good for him.

*　*　*　*　*

This was the pleasantest year of all the life I led in this place. Friday began to talk pretty well, and understand the names

[43]

of almost everything I had occasion to call for so that, in short, I began now to have some use for my tongue again, which indeed I had very little occasion for before. Besides the pleasure of talking to him, I had a singular satisfaction in the fellow himself. His simple unfeigned honesty appeared to me more and more every day, and I began really to love the creature. And, on his side, I believe he loved me more than it was possible for him ever to love anything before.

I had a mind once to try if he had any hankering inclination for his own country again, and having taught him English so well that he could answer me almost any questions, I asked him whether the nation that he belonged to never conquered in battle? At which he smiled and said, 'Yes, yes; we always fight the better.' That is, he meant always get the better in fight, and so we began the following discourse: 'You always fight the better,' said I. 'How came you to be taken prisoner then, Friday?'

Friday. My nation beat much, for all that.

Master. How beat? If your nation beat them, how come you to be taken?

Friday. They more many than my nation in the place where me was. They take one, two, three, and me. My nation over beat them in the yonder place, where me no was. There my nation take one, two, great thousand.

Master. But why did not your side recover you from the hands of your enemies then?

Friday. They run one, two, three, and me, and make go in the canoe. My nation have no canoe that time.

Master. Well, Friday, and what does your nation do with

the men they take? Do they carry them away and eat them, as these did?

Friday. Yes, my nation eat mans too, eat all up.

Master. Where do they carry them?

Friday. Go to other place where they think.

Master. Do they come hither?

Friday. Yes, yes, they come hither; come other else place.

Master. Have you been here with them?

Friday. Yes, I been here. (Points to the north-west side of the island, which it seems was their side.)

By this I understood that my man Friday had formerly been among the savages who used to come on shore on the farther part of the island on the said man-eating occasions that he had been brought for. And some time after, when I took the courage to take him to that side, he knew the place, and told me he was there once when they ate up twenty men, two women, and one child. He could not count twenty in English, but he numbered them by laying so many stones on a row, and pointing to me to tell them over.

I have told this passage because it introduces what follows. After I had this discourse with him, I then asked him how far it was from our island to the shore, and whether the canoes were not often lost? He told me there was no danger, no canoes were ever lost; but that, after a little way out to the sea, there was a current and a wind, always one way in the morning, the other in the afternoon.

This I understood to be no more than the sets of the tide, going out or coming in. I asked Friday a thousand questions about the country, the inhabitants, the sea, the coast, and what

In about a month's hard labour, we finished it

nations were near. He told me all he knew with the greatest
openness imaginable. I asked him the names of the several
nations of his sort of people, but could get no other name than
Caribs. He told me that up a great way beyond the moon, that
was, beyond the setting of the moon, which must be west
from their country, there dwelt white, bearded men like me,
and pointed to my great whiskers, which I mentioned before,
and that they had killed much mans — that was his word.
By all of which I understood he meant Spaniards, whose
cruelties in America had been spread over all the countries,
and were remembered by all the nations from father to son.

I inquired if he could tell me how I might go from this island,
and get among those white men. He told me, 'Yes, yes, I might

go in two canoe.' I could not understand what he meant or make him describe to me what he meant by two canoe, till at last, with great difficulty, I found he meant it must be in a large boat, as big as two canoes.

From this time I entertained some hopes that, one time or other, I might find an opportunity to make my escape from this place, and that this poor savage might be a means to help me to do it.

Without any more delay, I went to work with Friday to find a big enough great tree to fell, and make a large canoe to undertake the voyage. There were trees enough in the island to have built a little fleet, not of canoes, but even of good large vessels. But the main thing I looked for, was to get one so near the water that we might launch it when it was made.

At last Friday pitched upon a tree, for I found he knew much better than I what kind of wood was fittest for it. Nor can I tell, to this day, what wood to call the tree we cut down, except that it was very like the tree we call fustic, or between that and the Nicaragua wood. Friday was for burning the hollow or cavity of this tree out to make it into a boat, but I showed him how rather to cut it out with tools which, after I had showed him how to use, he did very handily. And in about a month's hard labour, we finished it, and made it very handsome, especially when with our axes, which I showed him how to handle, we cut and hewed the outside into the true shape of a boat. After this, however, it cost us near a fortnight's time to get her along, as it were, inch by inch upon great rollers into the water. But when she was in, she would have carried twenty men with great ease.

I was near two months performing the final work—namely

'Well, Friday,' says I, 'do not be frightened'

rigging and fitting my mast and sails, for I finished them very complete, making a small stay, and a sail or fore-sail to it, to assist if we should turn to windward.

The rainy season was in the meantime upon me, when I kept more within doors than at other times. So I had stowed our new vessel as secure as we could, bringing her up into the creek where, as I said in the beginning, I landed my rafts from the ship. Hauling her up to the shore at high-water mark, I made my man Friday dig a little dock. Then, when the tide was out, we made a strong dam across the end of it, to keep the water out, and so she lay, dry, as to the tide from the sea. To keep the rain off, we laid a great many boughs of trees so thick that she was as well thatched as a house, and thus we waited for the months of November and December, in which I planned to make my adventure.

When the settled season began to come in, I was preparing daily for the voyage. And the first thing I did was to lay by a certain quantity of provisions, being the stores for our voyage; and intended, in a week or a fortnight's time, to open the dock and launch out our boat. I was busy one morning upon something of this kind, when I called to Friday, and bid him go to the seashore and see if he could find a turtle or tortoise—a thing which we generally got once a week, for the sake of the eggs as well as the flesh. Friday had not been long gone, when he came running back, and flew over my outer wall or fence like one that felt not the ground or the steps he set his feet on. Before I had time to speak to him, he cried out to me, 'O master! O master!—O sorrow!—O bad!' 'What's the matter, Friday?' says I. 'O—yonder—there,' says he, 'one, two, three canoe! — one, two, three!' By his way of speaking I concluded there were six, but on enquiry, I found it was but three. 'Well, Friday,' says I, 'do not be frighted.' So I heartened him up as well as I could. However, I saw the poor fellow was most terribly scared, for nothing ran in his head but that they were come to look for him, and would cut him in pieces and eat him. The poor fellow trembled so, that I scarce knew what to do with him. I comforted him as well as I could, and told him I was in as much danger as he, and that they would eat me as well as him. 'But,' says I, 'Friday, we must resolve to fight them. Can you fight, Friday?' 'Me shoot,' says he, 'but there come many great number.' 'No matter for that,' said I again, 'our guns will fright them that we do not kill,' and I asked him,

A white man lay upon the beach with his hands and his feet tied

Whether, if I resolved to defend him, he would defend me, and stand by me, and do just as I bid him? He said, 'Me die, when you bid die, master.' So I went and fetched a good dram of rum to give him, for I had been so good a husband of my rum that I had a great deal left. When he had drunk it, I made him take the two fowling-pieces, which we always carried, and load them with large swan-shot, as big as small pistol bullets. Then I took four muskets, and loaded them with two slugs and five small bullets each, and my two pistols I loaded with a brace of bullets each. I hung my great sword as usual naked by my side, and gave Friday his hatchet.

When I had thus prepared myself, I took my telescope-glass, and went up to the side of the hill to see what I could discover.

And I found quickly, by my glass, that there were one-and-twenty savages, three prisoners, and three canoes, and that their whole business seemed to be the triumphal banquet uonn these three human bodies.

I observed, also, that they were landed, not where they had done when Friday made his escape, but nearer to my creek, where the shore was low, and where a thick wood came close almost down to the sea. This, with the abhorrence of the inhuman errand these wretches came about, filled me with such indignation, that I came down again to Friday and told him I was resolved to go down to them and kill them all.

With this resolution I entered the wood, and with all possible wariness and silence, Friday following close at my heels, I marched till I came to the edge of the wood, on the side which was next to them. Only one corner of the wood lay between me and them. Here I called softly to Friday, and showing him a great tree, which was just at the corner of the wood, I bade him go to the tree and bring me word if he could see there plainly what they were doing. He did so, and came immediately back to me and told me that they were all about their fire, eating the flesh of one of their prisoners. Another lay there bound upon the sand, a little from them, which he said they would kill next, and which fired all the very soul within me. He told me it was not one of their nation, but one of the bearded men he had told me of. I was filled with horror at the naming of the white-bearded man, and going to the tree I saw plainly by my glass a white man who lay upon the beach of the sea, with his hands and his feet tied with grasses, or things like rushes, and that he was a European, and had clothes on.

I had now not a moment to lose, for nineteen of the dreadful

So many were wounded that they ran about yelling and screaming

wretches sat upon the ground, all close huddled together, and had just sent the other two to butcher the poor Christian, and bring him perhaps limb by limb to their fire. They were now stooped down to untie the bands at his feet. I turned to Friday. 'Now, Friday,' said I, 'do as I bid thee.' Friday said he would. 'Then, Friday,' says I, 'do exactly as you see me do—fail in nothing.' So I set down one of the muskets and the fowling-piece upon the ground, and Friday did the like by his, and with the other musket I took my aim at the savages. Then asking him if he was ready, he said 'Yes.' 'Then fire at them,' said I, and at the same moment I fired also.

Friday took his aim so much better than I, that on the side

that he shot he killed two of them, and wounded three more. On my side, I killed one and wounded two. They were, as you may be sure, in a dreadful consternation, and all of them who were not hurt jumped up upon their feet, but did not immediately know which way to run or which way to look—for they knew not from whence their destruction came. Friday kept his eyes close upon me, that, as I had bid him, he might observe what I did. So as soon as the first shot was made I threw down the piece and took up the fowling-piece, and Friday did the like. 'Are you ready, Friday?' said I. 'Yes,' says he. 'Let fly, then,' says I, 'in the name of God!' and with that I fired again among the amazed wretches, and so did Friday. And as our pieces were now loaded with what I called swanshot, or small pistol bullets, we found only two drop but so many were wounded, that they ran about yelling and screaming, like mad creatures, all bloody and miserably wounded, most of them. Three more fell quickly after, though not quite dead.

'Now, Friday,' says I, laying down the discharged pieces, and taking up the musket which was yet loaded, 'follow me,' says I, which he did, with a great deal of courage. I rushed out of the wood and showed myself, Friday close at my foot. As soon as I perceived they saw me, I shouted as loud as I could, and bade Friday do so too, and running as fast as I could, I made directly towards the poor victim. The two butchers, who were just going to work with him, had left him at the surprise of our first fire, and fled in a fright to the sea and had jumped into a canoe, and three more of the rest made the same way. I turned to Friday, and bid him step forward and fire at them. He understood me, and running about forty yards to be near them, he shot at them. He killed two, and wounded

Three killed by the Spaniard

the third, so that he lay down in the bottom of the boat, as if he had been dead.

While my man Friday fired at them, I pulled out my knife and cut the reeds that bound the poor victim, and loosing his hands and feet, I lifted him up, and asked him in the Portuguese tongue, who he was. He answered in Latin, 'Christianus,' but was so weak and faint, that he could scarce stand or speak. I took my bottle out of my pocket and gave it him, making signs that he should drink, which he did. Then I asked him, 'What countryman he was?' And he said 'Espagniole', and being a little recovered, let me know, by all the signs he could possibly make, how much he was in my debt for his deliverance. 'Seignior,' said I, with as much Spanish as I could make up, 'we will talk afterwards, but we must fight now. If you have any strength left, take this pistol and sword and lay about you.' He took them very thankfully, and no sooner had he the arms in his hands but, as if they had put new vigour into him, he flew upon his murderers like a fury, and had cut two of them in pieces in an instant.

Friday, being now left to his liberty, pursued the flying wretches with no weapon in his hand but his hatchet, and with that he dispatched the rest he could come up with. And the Spaniard coming to me for a gun, I gave him one of the fowling-pieces, with which he pursued two of the savages, and wounded them both. But as he was not able to run, they both got from him into the wood, where Friday pursued them and killed one of them. But the other was too nimble for him, and though he was wounded, yet had plunged himself into the sea, and swam with all his might off to those three who were left in the canoe. The four in the canoe, with one wounded, who we know not whether he died or no, were all that escaped our hands of one-and-twenty. The account of the rest is as follows:

3 Killed at our first shot from the tree.
2 Killed at the next shot.
2 Killed by Friday in the boat.
2 Killed by ditto, of those at first wounded.
1 Killed by ditto, in the wood.
3 Killed by the Spaniard.
4 Killed, being found dropped here and there of their wounds, or killed by Friday in his chase of them.
4 Escaped in the boat, whereof one wounded, if not dead.
___
21 in all.

[55]

Gave the poor wretch a dram

Those that were in the canoe worked hard to get out of gunshot, and though Friday made two or three shots at them, I did not find that he hit any of them. Friday would fain have had me take one of their canoes, and pursue them. And indeed I was very anxious about their escape, lest carrying the news home to their people, they should come back, perhaps, with two or three hundred of their canoes, and devour us by mere multitude. So I consented to pursue them by sea, and running to one of their canoes, I jumped in, and bade Friday follow me. But when I was in the canoe I was surprised to find another poor creature lie there alive, bound hand and foot for the slaughter, and almost dead with fear, not knowing what the matter was.

I immediately cut the twisted reeds, or rushes, which they had bound him with, and would have helped him up. But he could not stand or speak, and groaned most piteously, believing that he was only unbound in order to be killed.

When Friday came to him, I bade him speak to him, and tell him of his deliverance, and pulling out my bottle, made him give the poor wretch a dram which, with the news of his being delivered, revived him, and he sat up in the boat. But when Friday came to hear him speak, and look in his face, it would have moved anyone to tears to have seen how Friday kissed him, embraced him, hugged him, cried, laughed, hallooed, jumped about, danced, sung, then cried again, wrung his hands, beat his own face and head, and then sung and jumped about again like a distracted creature. It was a good while before I could make him speak to me, but when he came to himself, he told me that it was his father.

This action put an end to our pursuit of the canoe with the other savages, who were now gotten almost out of sight. And it was happy for us that we did not, for it blew so hard within two hours after, and before they could be gotten a quarter of their way, and continued blowing so hard all night, that I could not suppose their boat could live.

* * * * *

My island was now peopled, and I thought myself very rich in subjects. And it was a merry reflection which I frequently made, how like a king I looked. First of all the whole country was my very own property, so that I had an undoubted right of dominion. Secondly, my people were perfectly subjected.

I was absolute lord and law-giver. They all owed their lives to me, and were ready to lay down their lives, if there had been occasion of it, for me. It was remarkable, too, we had but three subjects, and they were of three different religions. My man Friday was a Protestant, his father was a Pagan and cannibal, and the Spaniard was a Papist. However, I allowed liberty of conscience throughout my dominions. But this is by the way.

As soon as I had secured my two weak rescued prisoners, and given them shelter, I began to think of provisions for them. And the first thing I did, I ordered Friday to take a yearling goat out of my particular flock, to be killed, when I cut off the hinder quarter, and chopping it into small pieces, I set Friday to work to boiling and stewing. It made them a very good dish, I assure you, of flesh and broth, having put some barley and rice also into the broth. I sat down and ate my own dinner also with them, and, as well as I could, cheered them and encouraged them. Friday was my interpreter, especially to his father, and indeed to the Spaniard too, for the Spaniard spoke the language of the savages pretty well.

I then began to enter into a little conversation with my two new subjects. And first I set Friday to inquire of his father what he thought of the escape of the savages in that canoe, and whether we might expect a return of them with a power too great for us to resist. His first opinion was, that the savages in the boat never could live out the storm. But as to what they would do if they came safe on shore, he said he knew not. But it was his opinion that they were so dreadfully frighted with the manner of their being attacked—the noise and the fire—that he believed they would tell their people they were

I had a serious talk with the Spaniard

all killed by thunder and lightning, not by the hand of man, and that whoever went to that enchanted island would be destroyed with fire from the gods!

This, however, I knew not, and therefore kept always upon my guard.

In a little time, however, no more canoes appearing, the fear of their coming wore off, and I began to take my former thoughts of a voyage to the main into consideration.

I had a serious talk with the Spaniard, and understood that there were indeed sixteen more of his countrymen and Portuguese who, having been cast away and made their escape to the mainland, lived there at peace with the savages, but were very sore put to it for necessaries, and indeed for life.

The captain of the vessel and his officers marvelled at my strange appearance

I asked him how he thought they would receive a proposal from me which might tend towards an escape and whether, if they were all here, it might not be done? I told him very freely I feared mostly their treachery and ill-usage of me if I put my life in their hands.

He told me they were all of them very civil, honest men, and they were under the greatest distress imaginable, having neither weapons nor clothes nor any food, but at the mercy and discretion of the savages, out of all hopes of ever returning to their own country. He was sure that, if I would undertake their relief, they would live and die by me.

Upon these assurances, I resolved to venture to relieve them

It appeared to be an English ship

if possible, and to send the old savage and the Spaniard over
to them to treat. To this purpose I marked out several trees
which I thought fit for our work, and I set Friday and his
father to cutting them down, and then I caused the Spaniard,
to whom I imparted my thought on that affair, to oversee and
direct their work. I showed them with what indefatigable
pains I had hewed a large tree into single planks, and I caused
them to do the like, till they had made about a dozen large
planks of good oak, near two foot broad, thirty-five foot long,
and from two inches to four inches thick. What prodigious
labour it took up, anyone may imagine.

I gave the Spaniard leave to go over to the mainland to see

what he could do with those he had left behind there. I gave him a strict charge in writing not to bring any man with him who would not first swear in the presence of himself and of the old savage, that he would no way injure, fight with or attack the person he should find in the island, who was so kind to send for them in order to bring about their deliverance.

I gave each of them a musket with a firelock on it, and about eight charges of powder and ball, charging them not to use either of them except upon urgent occasion.

Under these instructions, the Spaniard and the old savage, the father of Friday, went away in one of the canoes which they might be said to come in, or rather were brought in, when they came as prisoners to be devoured by the savages.

★   ★   ★   ★   ★

They went away with a fair gale, on the day that the moon was at full, by my account in the month of October.

It was no less than eight days I waited for them, when a strange accident intervened, of which the like has not perhaps been heard of in history. I was fast asleep in my hutch one morning, when my good man Friday came running in to me and called aloud, 'Master, master, they are come, they are come!'

I jumped up and went out as soon as I could get my clothes on, through my little grove, which by the way, was by this time grown to be a very thick wood. I say, regardless of danger, for I went without my arms, which was not my custom, but I was surprised, when, turning my eyes to the sea, I presently saw a boat at about a league and a half's distance, standing in for the shore with a shoulder-of-mutton sail, as they used to call it.

Also I observed, presently, that they did not come from that side which the shore lay on, but from the southernmost end of the island. Upon this I called Friday in, and bid him lie close, for these were not the people we looked for, and we did not know yet whether they were our friends or enemies.

In the next place, I went in to fetch my telescope-glass to see what I could make of them, and having taken the ladder out, I climbed up to the top of the hill.

I had scarce set my foot on the hill, when my eye plainly discovered a ship lying at an anchor, at about a league and a half from the shore. By my observation it appeared to be an English ship, and the boat appeared to be an English long-boat.

I cannot express the confusion I was in, though the joy of seeing a ship, and one which I had reason to believe was manned by my own countrymen, was such as I cannot describe.

For the next few hours, in which time the crew of the long-boat filled up the ship's water-casks, this being the purpose for which they had put in to this unknown island, I was in a delirium of talk. The captain of the vessel and his officers marvelled at my strange appearance and the array of contrivances I could show to account for my long survival. And every question of theirs being in my own language was a delight to me to hear. Still talking we went aboard ship, the captain agreeing that my faithful man Friday should have passage with me.

When I took leave of this island I carried on board for relics the great goat-skin cap I had made, my umbrella, and my parrot.

Thus I left the island on the 19th December, as I found by the ship's account, in the year 1686, after I had been upon it eight and twenty years, two months, and nineteen days.

In this vessel, after a long voyage, I arrived in England the 11th of June, in the year 1687, having been thirty and five years absent.

TREASURE ISLAND

by

ROBERT LOUIS STEVENSON

I remember him as if it were yesterday, as he came plodding to the inn door, his sea chest following behind him in a hand-barrow, a tall, strong, heavy, nut-brown man, his tarry pigtail falling over the shoulders of his soiled blue coat, his hands ragged and scarred with black, broken nails, and the sabre-cut across one cheek, a dirty, vivid white.

'This is a handy cove,' he said, 'and a pleasant sittyated grog-shop. Much company, mate?'

My father, who owned the inn where we lived, told him no, very little company, the more was the pity.

'Well, then,' said he, 'this is the berth for me. Here you, matey,' he cried to the man who trundled the barrow; 'bring up alongside and help up my chest. I'll stay here a bit,' he continued. 'I'm a plain man; rum and bacon and eggs is what I want, and that headland up there for to watch the ships off. What might you call me? You might call me captain. Oh, I see what you're at — there;' and he threw down three or four gold pieces on the threshold. 'You can tell me when I've worked through that,' said he, looking as fierce as a commander.

And, indeed, bad as his clothes were, and coarsely as he spoke, he had none of the appearance of a man who sailed before the mast, but seemed like a mate or skipper accustomed to be obeyed or to strike. He was a very silent man by custom. All day he hung round the cove, or upon the cliffs with a brass telescope, all evening he sat in a corner of the parlour next the fire and drank rum and water very strong. Every day, when he came back from his stroll, he would ask if any sea-faring man had gone by along the road. At first we thought it was the want of company of his own kind that made him ask this question, but at last we began to see he was desirous to avoid them.

There were nights when he took a deal more rum and water than his head would carry, and then he would sometimes sit and sing wicked, old, wild sea-songs, minding nobody. But sometimes he would call for glasses all round, and force the trembling company to listen to his stories or join in a chorus to his singing. Often I have heard the house shaking with 'Yo-ho-ho, and a bottle of rum,' each man singing louder than the other, to avoid remark. For in these fits he was the most over-riding companion ever known. He would slap his hand on the table for silence all round; he would fly in a passion of anger at a question, or sometimes because none was put, he judged the company was not following his story. Nor would he allow

...came to the inn door, his sea chest following behind in a hand-barrov

anyone to leave the inn till he had drunk himself sleepy and reeled off to bed.

In one way, indeed, he bade fair to ruin us, for he kept on staying week after week, and at last month after month, so that all the money had been long exhausted, and still my father never plucked up the heart to insist on having more. If ever he mentioned it, the captain blew through his nose so loudly that you might say he roared, and stared my poor father out of the room.

He was only crossed once, and that towards the end, when my father was far gone in a decline that took him off. Dr. Livesey came late one afternoon to see the patient, and took a bit of dinner from my mother, and went into the parlour to smoke a pipe until his horse should come down from the hamlet.

Suddenly the captain, sitting far gone in rum, began to pipe up his eternal song:

> *Fifteen men on the dead man's chest —*
> *Yo-ho-ho, and a bottle of rum!*
> *Drink and the devil had done for the rest —*
> *Yo-ho-ho, and a bottle of rum!* !!

The captain gradually brightened up at his own music, and at last slapped his hand upon the table before him in a way that we all knew to mean silence. The voices stopped at once, all but Dr. Livesey's. He went on as before, speaking clear and kind, and drawing briskly at his pipe between every word or two. The captain glared at him for a while, slapped his hand again, glared still harder, and at last broke out with a villainous, low oath: 'Silence, there, between decks!'

'Were you addressing me, Sir? said the doctor, and when the ruffian had told him, with another oath, that this was so, 'I have only one thing to say to you, sir,' replied the doctor, 'that if you keep on drinking rum, the world will soon be quit of a very dirty scoundrel!'

The old fellow's fury was awful. He sprang to his feet, drew and opened a sailor's clasp knife, and, balancing it open on the palm of his hand, threatened to pin the doctor to the wall.

The doctor never so much as moved. He spoke to him as before, over his shoulder, and in the same tone of voice, rather high, so that all the room might hear, but perfectly calm and steady:

'If you do not put that knife this instant in your pocket, I promise, upon my honour, you shall hang at the next assizes.'

'*Silence, there, between decks!*'

Then followed a battle of looks between them, but the captain soon knuckled under, put up his weapon, and resumed his seat, grumbling like a beaten dog.

The doctor's words were prophetic. Soon afterwards the captain had a stroke and took to his bed. He still called for rum, however.

'Your doctor hisself said one glass wouldn't hurt me. I'll give you a golden sovereign for a noggin, Jim.'

'I want none of your money,' said I, 'but what you owe my father. I'll get you one glass, and no more.'

When I brought it to him he seized it greedily, and drank it out.

'Aye, aye,' said he, 'that's some better, sure enough. And now, matey, did that doctor say how long I was to lie here in this old berth?'

'A week, at least.'

'A week! I can't do that: they'll have the black spot on me by then. The lubbers is going about to get the wind of me this blessed moment. But I'll trick 'em again. I'll shake out another reef, matey, and daddle 'em again.'

As he was thus speaking, he had risen from bed with great difficulty, holding to my shoulder with a grip that almost made me cry out, and moving his legs like so much dead weight. His words, spirited as they were in meaning, contrasted sadly with the weakness of the voice in which they were uttered. He paused when he had got into a sitting position on the edge.

'That doctor's done me,' he murmured. 'My ears is singing. Lay me back.'

Before I could do much to help him he had fallen back again to his former place, where he lay for a while silent.

'Jim,' he said presently, 'if I can't get away nohow, and they tip me the black spot — mind you, it's my old sea chest they're after — you get on a horse — you can, can't you? Well then, you get on a horse, and go to—well yes, go to—to that infernal doctor swab, and tell him to pipe all hands—magistrates and sich, and he'll lay 'em aboard at the "Admiral Benbow" — all old Flint's crew, man and boy, all on 'em that's left. I was first mate, I was, old Flint's first mate, and I'm the on'y one as knows the place. He gave it me at Savannah, when he lay a-dying, like as if I was to now, you see. But you won't peach unless they get the black spot on me, or unless you see the seafaring man with one leg, Jim—him above all.'

'But what is the black spot, Captain?' I asked.

'That's a summons, mate. I'll tell you if they get that. But you keep your weather-eye open, Jim, and I'll share with you equals, upon my honour.'

[72]

'If they tip me the black spot, it's my old sea chest they're after'

He wandered a little longer, his voice growing weaker; but soon after I had given him his medicine, which he took like a child, with the remark, 'If ever a seaman wanted drugs, it's me.' He fell at last into a heavy, swoon-like sleep, in which I left him. What I should have done had all gone well I do not know. Probably I should have told this story to the doctor, for I was in mortal fear lest the captain should repent of his confessions and make an end of me. But as things fell out, my poor father died quite suddenly that evening, which put all other matters on one side. Our natural distress, the visits of the neighbours, the arranging of the funeral, and all the work of the inn to be carried on meanwhile, kept me so busy that I had scarcely time to think of the captain, far less to be afraid of him.

He got downstairs next morning, to be sure, and had his meals as usual, though he ate little, and had more, I am afraid, than his usual supply of rum, for he helped himself out of the bar, scowling and blowing through his nose, and no one dared to cross him. On the night before the funeral he was as drunk as ever and it was shocking, in that house of mourning, to hear him singing away at his ugly old sea-song. But, weak as he was, we were all in fear of death from him, and the doctor was suddenly taken up with a case many miles away, and was never near the house after my father's death.

So things passed until the day after the funeral. I was standing at the door for a moment, full of sad thoughts about my father, when I saw someone drawing slowly near along the road. He was plainly blind, for he tapped before him with a stick, and wore a great green shade over his eyes and nose, and he was hunched, as if with age or weakness, and wore a huge old tattered sea-cloak with a hood. He stopped a little from the inn, and raising his voice in an odd singsong, addressed the air in front of him:

'Will any kind friend inform a poor blind man, who has lost the precious sight of his eyes in the gracious defence of his native country, England, and God bless King George! — where or in what part of this country he may now be?'

'You are at the "Admiral Benbow", Black Hill Cove, my good man,' said I.

'I hear a voice,' said he —'a young voice. Will you give me your hand, my kind young friend, and lead me in?'

I held out my hand, and the horrible, soft-spoken, eyeless creature gripped it in a moment like a vice.

'Now, boy,' he said, 'take me in to the captain.'

'Sir,' said I, 'upon my word I dare not.'

'Oh,' he sneered, 'that's it! Take me in straight, or I'll break your arm.'

'You are at the "Admiral Benbow",' said I

And he gave it, as he spoke, a wrench that made me cry out.
'Lead me straight up to him, and when I'm in view, cry out,
"Here's a friend for you, Bill!" If you don't, I'll do this.'
With that he gave me a twitch that I thought would have made
me faint. I was so utterly terrified of the blind beggar that I
forgot my fear of the captain, and, as I opened the parlour
door, cried out the words he had ordered in a trembling
voice.

The poor captain raised his eyes, and at one look the rum
went out of him, and left him staring sober. The expression of
his face was not so much of terror as of mortal sickness.

'Now, Bill, sit where you are,' said the beggar. 'If I can't see,
I can hear a finger stirring. Business is business. Hold out your
left hand. Boy, take his left hand by the wrist, and bring it near
to my right.'

We both obeyed him to the letter, and I saw him pass something from the hollow of the hand that held his stick into the palm of the captain's, which closed upon it instantly.

'And now that's done,' said the blind man, and at the word he suddenly left hold of me, and, with incredible accuracy and nimbleness, skipped out of the parlour and into the road, where as I stood motionless, I could hear his stick go tap-tap-tapping into the distance.

It was some time before either I or the captain seemed to gather our senses, but at length he drew in his hand and looked sharply into the palm.

'Ten o'clock!' he cried. 'Six hours. We'll do them yet,' and he sprang to his feet.

Even as he did so, he reeled, put his hand to his throat, stood swaying for a moment, and then, with a peculiar sound, fell from his whole height, face foremost to the floor.

I ran to him, calling to my mother. But haste was all in vain. The captain had been struck dead by thundering apoplexy. It is a curious thing to understand, for I had certainly never liked the man, though of late I had begun to pity him, but as soon as I saw that he was dead, I burst into a flood of tears. It was the second death I had known, and the sorrow of the first was still fresh in my heart.

★　　★　　★　　★　　★

I lost no time, of course, in telling my mother all that I knew, and perhaps should have told her long before. We saw ourselves at once in a difficult and dangerous position; some of the captain's money — if he had any — was certainly due to us, and we meant to have it, but remembering the visit of the

We opened the door and were in full retreat

blind beggar, I thought it unlikely the old man's shipmates would be inclined to give up their booty in payment of the dead man's debts. So I slipped the bolt on the door, and while my mother got a candle I plucked up my courage and removed the key of the captain's chest from the cord round his neck. Then, holding each other's hands, my mother and I advanced into the little room the captain had occupied and where his box had stood since the day of his arrival.

It was like any other seaman's chest on the outside, the initial 'B' burned on the top of it with a hot iron, and the corners somewhat smashed and broken by long, rough usage.

'Give me the key,' said my mother, and though the lock was very stiff she had turned it and thrown back the lid in a twinkling.

A strong smell of tobacco and tar rose from the interior, but

[77]

nothing was to be seen on the top except a suit of very good clothes, carefully brushed and folded. Under that, the miscellany began — a quadrant, a tin canikin, several sticks of tobacco, two brace of very handsome pistols, a piece of bar silver, an old Spanish watch and some other trinkets of little value. Underneath an old boat-cloak there lay before us the last things in the chest, a bundle tied up in oilcloth and looking like papers, and a canvas bag that gave forth, at a touch, the jingle of gold.

'I'll show those rogues that I'm an honest woman,' said my mother. 'I'll have my dues, and not a farthing over. Hold the bag.' And she began to count over the amount of the captain's score from the sailor's bag into the one that I was holding.

When we were about half-way through, I suddenly put my hand upon her arm. For I had heard, in the silent, frosty night, a sound that brought my heart into my mouth—the tap-tapping of the blind man's stick upon the frozen road. It drew nearer and nearer, while we sat holding our breath. Then it struck sharp on the inn door, and then we could hear the handle being turned, and the bolt rattling as the wretched being tried to enter; and then there was a long time of silence both within and without. At last the tapping recommenced, and, to our inde-scribable joy and gratitude, died away slowly again until it ceased to be heard.

'Mother,' said I, 'take the whole and let's be going,' for I felt sure the bolted door must have seemed suspicious, and would bring the whole hornet's nest about our ears.

'I'll take what I have,' she said, jumping to her feet.

'I'll take this to square the account,' I said, picking up the oilskin packet.

The doctor opened the seals, and there fell out the map of an island

Next moment we were both groping downstairs, leaving the candle by the empty chest, and the next we had opened the front door and were in full retreat. We paused a few minutes by the bridge, as my poor mother felt faint, and, concealed by the bushes I witnessed the return of the blind beggar with several companions, who immediately broke down the door of the 'Admiral Benbow'. I only stayed long enough to hear their cries of surprise when they found that the captain was dead, and their oaths at discovering his chest had been opened, before guiding my mother to the nearest cottage for shelter.

* * * * *

That same night, after leaving my mother safe in the village, I went at once to Dr. Livesey's house. I was shown into a great library, where the squire and Dr. Livesey sat, pipe in hand, on either side of a bright fire.

'Good evening to you, friend Jim,' said the doctor, 'what good wind brings you here?'

I told my story like a lesson, and you should have seen how the two gentlemen leaned forward and looked at each other, and forgot to smoke in their interest and surprise.

'And so, Jim,' said the doctor, 'you have the thing that they were after, have you?'

'Here it is, sir,' said I, giving him the oilskin packet, and he put it quietly in the pocket of his coat.

'You have heard of this Flint, I suppose?'

'Heard of him!' cried the squire. 'Heard of him, you say! He was the bloodthirstiest buccaneer that sailed.'

'Well, I've heard of him myself, in England,' said the doctor. 'But the point is, had he money?'

'Money!' cried the squire. 'What were those villains after but money?'

'That we shall soon know,' replied the doctor. 'Supposing that I have here in my pocket some clue to where Flint buried his treasure, will that treasure amount to much?'

'Amount, sir!' cried the squire. 'It will amount to this. If we have the clue you talk of, I will fit out a ship in Bristol dock, and take you and Hawkins here along, and I'll have that treasure if I search a year.'

'Very well, then,' said the doctor. 'Now then, if Jim is agreeable, we'll open the packet,' and he laid it on the table.

The bundle was sewn together, and the doctor had to get out his instrument-case and cut the stitches with his medical scissors. It contained two things — a book and a sealed paper.

'First of all we'll try the book,' observed the doctor. He

I lay there trembling and listening

perused for some time in silence, then laid it down. 'Not much instruction there,' he remarked, as he passed on.

The doctor opened the seals with great care, and there fell out the map of an island, with latitude and longitude, soundings, names of hills, and bays and inlets, and every particular that would be needed to bring a ship to a safe anchorage upon its shores. It was about nine miles long and five across, shaped, you might say, like a fat dragon standing up, and had two fine, land-locked harbours, and a hill in the centre part marked 'The Spy-glass'. There were several additions of a later date; but, above all, three crosses of red ink—two on the north part of the island, one in the south-west, and, beside this last, in the same red ink, in a small, neat hand, very different from the captain's tottery characters, these words: 'Bulk of treasure here.'

[81]

Over on the back the same hand had written this further information:

'Tall tree, Spy-glass shoulder, bearing a point to N. of N.N.E.
'Ten feet, Skeleton Island E.S.E. and by E.
'The bar silver is in the north cache; you can find it by the trend of the east hummock, ten fathoms south of the black crag with the face on it.
'The arms are easy found, in the sand hill, N. point of north inlet cape, bearing E. and a quarter N.

'J. F.'

That was all, but brief as it was, and, to me, incomprehensible, it filled the squire and Dr. Livesey with delight.

'Livesey,' said the squire, 'you will give up this wretched practice at once. Tomorrow I start for Bristol. In three weeks' time — three weeks! — two weeks — ten days — we'll have the best ship, sir, and the choicest crew in England. Hawkins shall come as cabin-boy. You'll make a famous cabin-boy, Hawkins. You, Livesey, are ship's doctor: I am admiral. We'll take my men, Redruth, Joyce, and Hunter. We'll have favourable winds, a quick passage, and not the least difficulty in finding the spot, and money to eat — to roll in — to play ducks and drakes with ever after.'

★　　★　　★　　★　　★

The squire was as good as his word: some weeks later, on being sent for, I went aboard his ship, the *Hispaniola*.

All that night we were in a bustle getting things stowed in their place, and boatloads of the squire's friends, Mr. Blandly

The lookout shouted, 'Land ho!'

and the like, coming off to wish him a good voyage and a safe return. We never had a night at the 'Admiral Benbow' when I had half the work, and I was dog-tired when, a little before dawn, the boatswain sounded his pipe, and the crew began to man the capstan-bars. I might have been twice as weary, yet I would not have left the deck, all was so new and interesting to me — the brief commands, the shrill note of the whistle, the men bustling to their places in the glimmer of the ship's lanterns.

'Now, Barbecue, tip us a stave,' cried a voice, addressing the cook.

'The old one,' cried another.

'Aye, aye, mates,' said the cook, who was standing by, with his crutch under his arm; and at once broke out in the air and words I knew so well:

Fifteen men on a dead man's chest —
And then the whole crew joined in the chorus:
Yo-ho-ho, and a bottle of rum!

The chorus at once reminded me of the captain, and of his fear of a one-legged seaman. Could this one-legged sea cook, Long John Silver, be the man? Our voyage was fairly prosperous, the captain and crew proving themselves very capable, but when we were drawing close to Treasure Island, I was un-wittingly to overhear some exceedingly disturbing news, and it happened like this.

One day, when I was on my way to my berth, it occurred to me that I would like an apple. I ran on deck, and unobserved by anyone got bodily into the apple-barrel, and found that there was scarce an apple left but, sitting down there in the dark, what with the sound of the waters and the rocking movement of the ship, I had either fallen asleep, or was on the point of doing so, when a heavy man sat down with rather a crash close by. The barrel shook as he leaned his shoulders against it, and I was just about to jump up when the man began to speak. It was Silver's voice, and, before I had heard a dozen words, I would not have shown myself for all the world. I lay there, trembling and listening, in the extreme of fear and curiosity, for from these dozen words I understood that the lives of all the honest men aboard depended upon me alone.

*   *   *   *   *

'No, not I,' said Silver. 'Flint was cap'n; I was quartermaster along of my timber leg.'

'Ah!' cried another voice, that of the youngest hand on board,

This was not the map we found in the captain's chest

was evidently full of admiration, 'he was the flower of the flock, was Flint!'

'This is the way of gentlemen of fortune,' said Silver. 'They live rough, and they risk swinging, but they eat and drink like fighting-cocks, when a cruise is done. Why, it's hundreds of pounds instead of hundreds of farthings in their pockets.'

'Well, I tell you now,' replied the lad, 'I didn't half a quarter like the job till I had this talk with you, John; but there's my hand on it now.'

'And a brave lad you were, and smart, too,' answered Silver, shaking hands so heartily that all the barrel shook, 'and a finer figurehead for a gentleman of fortune I never clapped my eyes on.'

By this time I had begun to understand the meaning of their terms. By a 'gentleman of fortune' they plainly meant neither more nor less than a common pirate, and the little scene that I had overheard was the last act in the corruption of one of the honest hands — perhaps of the last one left aboard. But on this point I was not to know the answer just yet for, Silver giving a little whistle, a third man strolled up and sat down by the party.

'Dick's square,' said Silver.

'Oh, I know'd Dick was square,' returned the voice of the coxswain, Israel Hands. 'He's no fool, is Dick. But look here,' he went on, 'here's what I want to know, Barbecue; when do we take over, eh?'

'When, by the powers!' cried Silver. 'Well, now, if you want to know, I'll tell you when. The last moment I can manage, and that's when. Here's a first-class seaman, Cap'n Smollett, sails the blessed ship for us. Here's this squire and doctor with a map and such—I don't know where it is, do I? No more do you, says you. Well then, I mean this squire and doctor shall find the stuff and help us to get it aboard, by the powers. I'll finish with 'em at the island, as soons' the treasure's on board—'

Suddenly the lookout shouted, 'Land ho!' and at once there was a great rush of feet across the deck. In the confusion, I slipped from my barrel, and came out upon the open deck in time to join Hunter and Dr. Livesey in the rush for the weather-bow.

There all hands were already congregated. A belt of fog had lifted almost simultaneously with the appearance of the moon. Away to the south-west of us we saw two hills, about a couple of miles apart, and rising behind them a third and higher hill, whose peak was still buried in the fog. All three seemed sharp and conical in shape.

So much I saw, almost in a dream, for I had not yet recovered from my horrid fear of a minute or two before. And then I heard the voice of Captain Smollett issuing orders. The *Hispaniola* was laid a couple of points nearer the wind, and now sailed a course that would just clear the island on the east.

'And now, men,' said the Captain, when all was sheeted home, 'has any one of you ever seen that land ahead?'

'I have, sir,' said Silver. 'I've watered there with a trader I was cook in.'

'The anchorage is on the south, behind an islet, I fancy?' asked the captain.

'Yes, sir: Skeleton Island they calls it.'

'I have a chart here,' says Captain Smollett. 'See if that's the place.'

Long John's eyes burned in his head as he took the chart; but, by the fresh look of the paper, I knew he was doomed to disappointment. This was not the map we had found in the captain's chest, but an accurate copy complete in all things—names and heights and soundings — with the single exception of the red crosses and the written notes. Sharp as must have been his annoyance, Silver had the strength of mind to hide it.

'Yes, sir,' he said, 'this is the spot to be sure; and very prettily drawn out. Who might have done that, I wonder? The pirates were too ignorant, I reckon. Aye, here it is, "Capt. Kidd's Anchorage" — just the name my shipmate called it. There's a strong current runs along the south, and then away nor'ard up the west coast. Right you was, sir,' says he, 'to haul your wind and keep the weather of the island.'

'Thank you, my man,' says Captain Smollett. 'I'll ask you, later on, to give us a help. You may go.'

Captain Smollett, the squire, and Dr. Livesey were talking together on the quarter-deck, and, anxious as I was to tell them my story, I durst not interrupt them openly. While I was still casting about in my thoughts to find a probable excuse, Dr. Livesey called me to his side. I broke out immediately: 'Doctor, let me speak. Get the captain and squire down to the cabin, and then make some pretence to send for me. I have terrible news!'

The doctor changed countenance a little, but next moment he was master of himself.

'Thank you, Jim,' he said, quite loudly, 'that was all I wanted to know,' as if he had asked me a question.

And with that he turned on his heel and rejoined the other two. They spoke together for a little, and though none of them started, or raised his voice, or so much as whistled, it was plain enough that Dr. Livesey had communicated my request, for the three gentlemen went below, and not long after, word was sent forward that Jim Hawkins was wanted in the cabin.

I found them all three seated round the table, a bottle of Spanish wine and some raisins before them, and the doctor smoking away, with his wig on his lap, and that, I knew, was a sign that he was agitated.

'Now, Hawkins,' said the squire, 'you have something to say. Speak up.'

I did as I was bid, and, as short as I could make it, told all the details of Silver's conversation. Nobody interrupted me until I was done, nor did any one of the three of them make so much as a movement, but they kept their eyes upon my face from first to last.

'Jim,' said Dr. Livesey, 'take a seat.'

We brought up just where the anchor was on the chart

And they made me sit down at table beside them, poured me out a glass of wine, filled my hands with raisins, and all three, one after the other, and each with a bow, drank my good health, and their service to me, for my luck and courage.

'You, sir, are the captain. It is for you to speak,' says Mr. Trelawney grandly, addressing Captain Smollett.

'First point,' began Captain Smollett, 'we must go on, because we can't turn back. If I gave the word to go about, they would rise at once. Second point, we have time before us — at least, until this treasure is found. Third point, there are some faithful hands. Now, sir, it's got to come to blows sooner or later, and what I propose is, to take time by the forelock, as the saying is, and come to blows some fine day when they least expect it. We can count, I take it, on your own home servants, Mr. Trelawney?'

'As upon myself,' declared the squire.

'Three,' reckoned the captain, 'ourselves making seven, counting Hawkins, here. Now, about the honest hands?'

'Most likely Trelawney's own men,' said the doctor; 'those he had picked up for himself, before he lit on Silver.'

'Well, gentlemen,' said the captain, 'the best that I can say is not much. We must lay-to, if you please, and keep a bright lookout. It's trying on a man, I know. It would be pleasanter to come to blows. But there's no help for it till we know our men. Lay-to, and whistle for a wind, that's my view.'

'Jim here,' said the doctor, 'can help us more than anyone. The men are not shy with him, and Jim is a noticing lad.'

'Hawkins, I put great faith in you,' added the squire.

I began to feel pretty desperate at this, for I felt altogether helpless; and yet, by an odd train of circumstances, it was indeed through me that safety came. In the meantime, talk as we pleased, there were only seven out of the twenty-six on whom we knew we could rely, and out of these seven one was a boy, so that the grown men on our side were six to their nineteen.

*   *   *   *   *

We brought up just where the anchor was on the chart, about a third of a mile from either shore, the mainland on one side, and Skeleton Island on the other. The bottom was clean sand. The plunge of our anchor sent up clouds of birds wheeling and crying over the woods, but in less than a minute they were down again, and all was once more silent.

The place was entirely land-locked, buried in woods, the trees coming right down to high-water mark, the shores mostly

I caught a branch and swung myself out

flat, and the hill-tops grouped round, one here, one there.
Two little rivers, or rather, two swamps, emptied out into this
pond, as you might call it, and the foliage on that part of the
shore had a poisonous brightness. A peculiar stagnant smell
hung over the anchorage — a smell of sodden leaves, and
rotting tree-trunks. I observed the doctor sniffing and spitting,
like someone tasting a bad egg.

'I don't know about treasure,' he said, 'but I'll stake my wig
there's fever here.'

The men lay about the deck together looking surly. The
slightest order was received with a black look, and grudgingly
and carelessly obeyed. Even the honest hands must have caught
the infection, for there was not one man better than another.
Mutiny, it was plain, hung over us like a thunder-cloud.

And it was not only we of the cabin party who perceived the danger. Long John was hard at work going from group to group, spending himself in good advice, and no man could have shown them a better example. He fairly outstripped himself in willingness and civility; he was all smiles to everyone. If an order were given, John would be on his crutch in an instant, with the cheeriest 'Aye, aye, sir!' in the world, and when there was nothing else to do, he kept up one song after another, as if to conceal the discontent of the rest.

Of all the gloomy features of that gloomy afternoon, this obvious anxiety on the part of Long John appeared the worst.

We held a council in the cabin.

'Sir,' said the captain, 'if I risk another order the whole ship'll come about our ears by the run. Now, we've only one man to rely on.'

'And who is that?' asked the squire.

'Silver, sir,' returned the captain, 'he's as anxious as you and I to smother things up. Let's allow the men an afternoon ashore. If they all go, why, we'll fight with the ship. If they none of them go, well then, we'll hold the cabin, and God defend the right. If some of 'em go, you mark my words, sir, Silver'll bring 'em aboard again as mild as lambs.'

It was so decided: loaded pistols were served out to all the sure men. Hunter, Joyce and Redruth were taken into our confidence, and received the news with less surprise and a better spirit than we had looked for. Then the captain went on deck and addressed the crew.

'My lads,' he said, 'a turn ashore'll hurt nobody—the boats are in the water. You can take the gigs, and as many as please can go ashore for the afternoon.'

A figure leapt behind the trunk of a pine

I believe the silly fellows must have thought they would break their shins over treasure as soon as they were landed, for they all came out of their sulks in a moment, and gave a cheer that started an echo in a faraway hill.

The captain was too clever to be in their way. He whipped out of sight in a moment, leaving Silver to arrange the party. Of the nineteen suspected mutineers, six were to stay on board, and the remaining thirteen, including Silver, began to embark.

Then it was that there came into my head the first of the mad notions that contributed so much to the saving of our lives. If six men were left by Silver, it was plain our party could not take and fight the ship; and since only six were left, it was equally plain that the cabin party had no present need of my assistance. It occurred to me at once to go ashore. In a jiffy

I had slipped over the side, and curled up in the fore-sheets of the nearest boat, and almost at the same moment she shoved off.

No one took any notice of me, only the bow oar saying,' Is that you, Jim? Keep your head down.' But Silver, from the other boat, looked sharply over and called out to know if that were me, and from that moment I began to regret what I had done.

The crews raced for the beach, but the boat I was in, having some start, and being at once the lighter and the better manned, shot far ahead of her consort, and the bow had struck among the trees, and I had caught a branch and swung myself out, and plunged into the nearest thicket, while Silver and the rest were still a hundred yards behind.

'Jim, Jim!' I heard him shouting.

But as you may suppose, I paid no heed. Jumping, ducking, and breaking through, I ran straight before my nose, till I could run no longer.

*　　*　　*　　*　　*

I was so pleased at having given the slip to Long John, that I began to enjoy myself and felt for the first time the joy of exploration. The isle was uninhabited, My shipmates I had left behind, and nothing lived in front of me but dumb brutes and fowls. I turned hither and thither among the trees. Here and there were flowering plants, unknown to me; here and there I saw snakes, and one raised his head from a ledge of rock and hissed at me with a noise not unlike the spinning of a top. Little did I suppose that he was a deadly enemy, and that the noise was the famous rattle of a rattle snake.

[94]

He was holding me by the wrist

As I made for the hill, which was steep and stony, some gravel became dislodged, and fell rattling and bounding across the ground to my feet. My eyes turned instinctively to the direction from which it had come, and I saw a figure leap with great rapidity behind the trunk of a pine. What it was, whether bear or man or monkey, I could in no way tell. It seemed dark and shaggy; more I knew not. But the terror of this apparition brought me to a stand. From trunk to trunk the creature flitted like a deer, running manlike on two legs, but unlike any man I had ever seen, stooping almost double as it ran. Yet it was a man; I could no longer be in doubt about that.

He was concealed by this time behind another tree trunk, but he must have been watching me closely, for as soon as I began to move in his direction he reappeared and took a step to meet me. Then he hesitated, drew back, came forward again, and at

[95]

last, to my wonder and confusion, threw himself on his knees at my feet, holding out his clasped hands to me.

At that I once more stopped.

'Who are you?' I asked.

'Ben Gunn,' he answered, and his voice sounded hoarse and awkward, like a rusty lock. 'I'm poor Ben Gunn, I am, and I haven't spoke with a Christian these three years.'

I could now see that he was a white man like myself, and that his features were even pleasing. His skin, wherever it was exposed, was burnt by the sun; even his lips were black, and his fair eyes looked quite startling in so dark a face. He was clothed with tatters of old ship's canvas and old sea-cloth, and this extraordinary patchwork was all held together by a system of the most various and incongruous fastenings, brass buttons, bits of stick, and loops of tarry twine. About his waist he wore an old brass-buckled leather belt, which was the one thing solid in his whole outfit.

'Three years!' I cried. 'Were you shipwrecked?'

'Nay, mate,' said he '—marooned.'

I had heard the word, and I knew it stood for a horrible kind of punishment common enough among the buccaneers, in which the offender is put ashore with a little powder and shot, and left behind on some desolate and distant island.

'Marooned three years ago,' he continued, 'and lived on goats since then, and berries, and oysters. Wherever a man is, says I, a man can do for himself. But, mate, my heart is sore for Christian diet. You mightn't happen to have a piece of cheese about you, now? No? Well, many's the long night I've dreamed of cheese—toasted, mostly—and woke up again, and here I were.'

I beheld the Union Jack flutter in the air

'If ever I get aboard again,' said I, 'you shall have cheese by the stone.'

'If ever you can get aboard again, says you?' he repeated. 'Why, now, who's to hinder you?'

'Not you, I know,' was my reply.

'And right you was,' he cried. 'Now you—what do you call yourself, mate?'

'Jim,' I told him.

'Jim, Jim,' says he, quite pleased apparently. 'Well, now, Jim, I've lived that rough as you'd be ashamed to hear of. Now, for instance, you wouldn't think I had had a pious mother—to look at me?' he asked.

'Why, no, not in particular,' I answered.

'Ah, well,' said he, 'but I had—*remarkable* pious. It were Providence that put me here. I've thought it all out in this here lonely island, and I'm back on piety. You don't catch me tasting rum so much, but just a thimbleful for luck, of course, the first chance I have. I know that I'll be good, and I can see the way to it. And, Jim'— looking all round him and lowering his voice to a whisper — 'I'm rich.'

I now felt sure that the poor fellow had gone crazy in his solitude, and I suppose I must have shown the feeling in my face, for he repeated the statement hotly:

'Rich! Rich! I says. And I'll tell you what, I'll make a man of you, Jim. Ah, Jim, you'll bless your stars, you will, you was the first that found me!'

And at this there came suddenly a lowering shadow over his face, and he tightened his grasp upon my hand, and raised a forefinger threateningly before my eyes.

'Now, Jim, you tell me true; that ain't Flint's ship?' he asked.

At this I had a happy inspiration. I began to believe that I had found an ally, and I answered him at once.

'It's not Flint's ship, and Flint's dead; but I'll tell you true, as you ask me to—there are some of Flint's old shipmates aboard.'

'Not a man—with one—leg?' he gasped.

'Silver?'

'Ah, Silver!' says he; 'that were his name.'

'He's the cook; and the ringleader, too.'

He was still holding me by the wrist, and at that he gave it a wring.

'If you were sent by Long John,' he said, 'I'm as good as pork, and I know it. But you wasn't, I don't suppose?'

I made up my mind in a moment, and by way of answer told him the whole story of our voyage, and the predicament in which we found ourselves. He heard me with the keenest interest, and when I had done he patted me on the head.

'You're a good lad, Jim,' he said, 'and you're all in a clove hitch, ain't you? Well, you just put your trust in Ben Gunn—Ben Gunn's the man to do it. Would you think it likely, now, that your squire would prove a liberal-minded one in case of help—him being in a clove hitch, as you remark?'

I told him the squire was the most generous of men.

'Aye, but you see,' returned Ben Gunn, 'what I mean is, would he be likely to come down to the tune of, say, one thousand pounds out of money that's as good as a man's own already?'

'I am sure he would,' said I. 'As it was, all hands were to share.' Upon hearing this he seemed very much relieved.

'Now I'll tell you what,' he went on. 'So much I'll tell you and no more. I were in Flint's ship when he buried the treasure!

'Three years later when I was in another ship, we sighted this very island. "Boys," said I, "here's Flint's treasure; let's land and find it." The captain was displeased at that, but all my messmates were of a mind, and we landed. Twelve days we looked for it, and every day they had the worse word for me, until one fine morning all hands went aboard. "As for you, Benjamin Gunn," says they, "here's a musket, and a spade, and pickaxe. You can stay here, and find Flint's money for yourself," they says.'

'Well, Jim, three years have I been here and—What's that?' he broke off.

For just then all the echoes of the island awoke and bellowed to the thunder of a cannon.

'They have begun to fight!' I cried. 'Follow me.'

[99]

I began to run towards the anchorage, my terrors all forgotten while, close at my side, the marooned man in his goatskins trotted easily and lightly.

'Left, left,' says he; 'keep to your left hand, mate Jim! Under the trees with you!'

The cannon-shot was followed, after a considerable interval, by the sound of a volley of small arms fire.

Another pause, and then, not a quarter of a mile in front of me, I beheld the Union Jack fluttering in the air above a wood.

★   ★   ★   ★   ★

As soon as Ben Gunn saw the colours he came to a halt, stopped me by the arm, and sat down.

'Now,' said he, 'there's your friends, sure enough.'

'Far more likely it's the mutineers,' I answered.

'What!' he cried. 'Why, in a place like this, where nobody puts in but gen'lemen of fortune, Silver would fly the Jolly Roger, you don't make no doubt of that. No, that's your friends. There's been blows, too, and I reckon your friends has had the best of it, and here they are ashore in the old stockade, as was made years and years ago by Flint.'

'Well,' said I, 'that may be so, and so be it; all the more reason that we should hurry on and join my friends.'

'Nay, mate,' returned Ben, 'not me. You're a good boy, or I'm mistook, but you're on'y a boy, all told. Now, Ben Gunn is fly. Rum wouldn't bring me there, where you're going—not rum wouldn't, till I see your born gen'leman, and gets it on his word of honour. And when Ben Gunn is wanted, you know where to find him, Jim. Just where you found him to-day, by the White Rock. And him that comes is to have a white thing in his hand, and he's to come alone.'

'Well,' said I, 'I believe I understand. You have something to propose, and you wish to see the squire or the doctor, and you're to be found where I found you. Is that all?'

'You won't forget?' he inquired, anxiously.

Here we were interrupted by a loud report, and a cannon ball came tearing through the trees and pitched in the sand, not a hundred yards from where we two were talking. The next moment each of us had taken to his heels in a different direction.

For a good hour to come frequent reports shook the island, and balls kept crashing through the woods. I moved from hiding-place to hiding-place, always pursued, or so it seemed to me, by these terrifying missiles. But towards the end of the bombardment, though I was still afraid to venture in the direction of the stockade, where the balls fell oftenest, I had begun, in a manner, to pluck up my heart again; and after a long detour to the east, crept down among the shore-side trees.

The *Hispaniola* still lay where she had anchored; but, sure enough, there was the Jolly Roger—the black flag of piracy— flying from her peak. Even as I looked, there came another red flash and another report that sent the echoes clattering, and one more round-shot whistled through the air. It was the last of the cannonade.

I decided to return towards the stockade.

I skirted among the woods and approached the stockade from the rear, or shoreward side. I found, in a clearing among the trees, a roughly-constructed, but sturdy log hut, completely enclosed by a high, strong fence. I climbed over with some difficulty, and was soon welcomed by the faithful party. In the

Another attack began

little hut there was, of course, Squire Trelawny and the doctor, in conversation with Captain Smollett; Redruth, Joyce and Hunter, Mr. Trelawny's own men, and Abraham Gray the ship's carpenter, a good young man at heart, who had decided to throw in his lot with us instead of with the rascally mutineers. This made our little party just seven men strong, or eight including myself.

I had soon told my story, and wanted to hear theirs. But the doctor had been thinking.

'Is this Ben Gunn a madman?' he asked.

'I do not know, sir,' I said. 'I am not very sure whether he's sane.'

'If there's any doubt about the matter, he is,' returned the doctor. 'Was it cheese you said he had a fancy for?'

'Yes, sir, cheese,' I answered.

'Well, Jim,' said he, 'you've seen my snuff-box, haven't you? And you never saw me take snuff, the reason being that in my snuff-box I carry a piece of Parmesan cheese—a cheese made in Italy, very nutritious. Well, that's for Ben Gunn.'

The squire now related how Captain Smollett, fearing that they would be trapped aboard the *Hispaniola*, had led his party ashore and seized the stockade. Using the jolly boat, they had brought ashore a supply of muskets and powder, some bread and biscuit, several kegs of pork, a cask of cognac, and also a very important item, the doctor's medicine chest. Though attacked by cannon and by direct assault, they had held out so far, and reduced the odds against them. It seemed, therefore, that our best hope was to kill off as many of the buccaneers as we could until they gave up and sailed away.

As Mr. Trelawney stated this conclusion, and the doctor nodded his agreement, another attack began. Suddenly, with a loud huzza, a little cloud of pirates leaped from the woods on the north side, and ran straight towards the stockade. At the same moment the fire was once more opened from the woods, and a rifle ball sang through the doorway, and knocked the doctor's musket into bits.

The boarders swarmed over the fence like monkeys. Squire and Gray fired again and yet again; three men fell, one forward into the enclosure, two back on the outside.

Two had bitten the dust, one had fled, four had made good their footing inside our defences, while from the shelter of the woods seven or eight men, each evidently supplied with several muskets, kept up a hot though useless fire on the log-house.

The four who had successfully climbed the fence made

'Fight 'em in the open!' cried the captain

straight before them for the building, shouting as they ran, and the men among the trees shouted back to encourage them. Several shots were fired, but such was the hurry of the marksmen, that not one appeared to have taken effect. In a moment, the four pirates had swarmed up the mound and were upon us.

The log-house was full of smoke, to which we owed our comparative safety. Cries and confusion, the flashes and reports of pistol shots, and one loud groan, rang in my ears.

'Out, lads, out, and fight 'em in the open! Cutlasses!' cried the captain.

I snatched a cutlass from the pile, and turned east. With my cutlass raised, I ran round the corner of the house. Next moment I was face to face with the boatswain. He roared aloud, and his cutlass went up above his head, flashing in the sunlight. I had not time to be afraid, but, as the blow still hung impending, leaped in a trice upon one side, and missing my foot in the soft sand, rolled headlong down the slope.

When I had first sallied from the door, the other mutineers had been already swarming up the palisade to make an end of us. One man, in a red night-cap, with his cutlass in his mouth, had even got upon the top and thrown a leg across. Well, so short had been the interval, that when I found my feet again, all were in the same posture, the fellow in the red cap still halfway over, another still just showing his head above the top of the stockade. And yet, in this breath of time, the fight was over, and the victory was ours.

Gray, following close behind me, had cut down the big boatswain before he had time to recover from his lost blow. Another had been shot at a loophole in the very act of firing into the house, and now lay in agony, the pistol still smoking in his hand. A third the doctor had disposed of at a blow. Of the four who had scaled the palisade, one only remained unaccounted for, and he, having left his cutlass on the field, was now clambering out again with the fear of death upon him.

'Fire—fire from the house!' cried the doctor. 'And you, lads, back into cover.'

But his words were unheeded, no shot was fired, and the last pirate made good his escape, and disappeared with the rest into the wood.

In three seconds nothing remained of the attacking party but the five who had fallen, four on the inside, and one on the outside, of the palisade.

The doctor and Gray and I ran full speed for shelter. The

survivors would soon be back where they had left their muskets, and at any moment the fire might recommence.

Inside the hut we found that Captain Smollett had been wounded in the shoulder, and although his condition was not serious, he was in considerable pain; and Squire Trelawny wept when he told me that two of his faithful servants, Redruth and Hunter, had been killed in the fighting. Whilst the doctor attended to the captain's wound, there was plenty of work for the rest of us. We buried the bodies of Redruth and Hunter, then prepared a meal of pork and bread. Mercifully there were no further attacks that day, and we spent a quiet, though uneasy night in the hut.

The next morning was spent by the squire and the doctor sitting by Captain Smollett's side, deep in consultation.

When they had talked to their hearts' content, it being then a little past noon, the doctor took up his hat and pistols, equipped himself with a cutlass, put the chart in his pocket, and with a musket over his shoulder, crossed the palisade on the north side, and set off briskly through the trees.

Gray and I were sitting together at the far end of the blockhouse, to be out of ear-shot of our officers' consulting, and Gray took his pipe out of his mouth and fairly forgot to put it back again, so thunderstruck was he at this occurrence.

'In the name of Davy Jones,' said he, 'is Dr. Livesey mad?'

'Why, no,' says I. 'He's about the last of this crew for that.'

'Well, shipmate,' said Gray, 'mad he may not be, but if *he's* not, you mark my words, *I* am.'

'I take it,' replied I, 'the doctor has an idea, and if I am right, he's going now to see Ben Gunn.'

I was right, as appeared later but, in the meantime, the

...in the centre of the dell was a little tent

house being stifling hot, and the little patch of sand inside the palisade ablaze with midday sun, I began to get another thought into my head. Why not, with Ben Gunn's help, have a try at cutting the *Hispaniola* adrift to go ashore where she fancied and so leave the pirates without a vessel? The others were busy helping the captain with his bandages and the coast was clear. I made a bolt for it over the stockade and into the thickest of the trees, before my absence was observed.

The white rock was visible enough above the brush, but it took me a goodish while to get up to it, crawling often on all fours among the scrub. Night had almost come when I laid my hands on its rough sides. Right below it there was an exceedingly small hollow of green turf, hidden by banks and a thick underbrush about knee-deep, that grew there very plentifully. In the centre of the dell, sure enough, was a little tent

[107]

of goatskins, like those the gipsies carry about with them in England. There was no sign of Ben himself, or of Dr. Livesey.

I dropped into the hollow, lifted the side of the tent and there was a coracle—home made if ever anything was home made—a rude, lopsided framework of tough wood, and stretched upon it a covering of goatskin, with the hair inside. The thing was extremely small, even for me, and I could hardly imagine that it could have floated with a full-sized man. There was one seat set across as low as possible, a kind of stretcher in the bows, and a double paddle for propulsion. I shouldered the coracle, and stumbled out of the hollow down to the sea.

The ebb had already run some time, and I had to wade through a long belt of swamp sand, where I sank several times above the ankle, before I came to the edge of the retreating water and, wading a little way in, set my coracle, keel down-wards, on the surface. By now it was quite dark.

*   *   *   *   *

The coracle—as I had ample reason to know before I was done with her—was a very safe boat for a person of my height and weight, both buoyant and clever in a seaway, but she was the most cross-grained, lop-sided craft to manage. Do as you pleased, she always made more leeway than anything else, and turning round and round was the manoeuvre she was best at. Even Ben Gunn himself has since admitted that she was 'queer to handle till you knew her way'.

Certainly I did not know her way. She turned in every direction but the one I wanted to go. The most part of the time we were broadside on, and I am very sure I never should have made the ship at all but for the tide. By good fortune, paddle as I pleased, the tide was still sweeping me down, and there lay the *Hispaniola* right in the fairway, hardly to be missed.

First she loomed before me like a blot of something yet blacker than darkness, then her spars and hull began to take shape and the next moment as it seemed (for, the further I went, the brisker grew the current of the ebb) I was alongside of her hawser and had laid hold.

The hawser was as taut as a bowstring, so strong she pulled upon her anchor. All round the hull, in the blackness, the rippling current bubbled and chattered like a little mountain stream. One cut with my knife and the *Hispaniola* would go humming down the tide.

So far so good, but it next occurred to my recollection that a taut hawser, suddenly cut, is a thing as dangerous as a kicking horse. Ten to one, if I were so foolhardy as to cut the *Hispaniola* from her anchor, I and the coracle would be knocked clean out of the water. While I was meditating, a puff came, caught the *Hispaniola* ,and forced her up into the current, and to my great joy I felt the hawser slacken in my grasp, and the hand by which I held it dip for a second under water.

With that I made up my mind, took out my knife, opened it with my teeth, and cut one strand after another till the vessel only swung by two. Then I lay quiet, waiting to sever the last when the strain should be once more lightened by a breath of wind.

All this time I had heard the sound of loud voices from the cabin. One I recognized for the coxswain's, Israel Hands, who had been Flint's gunner in former days, the other was my friend of the red nightcap. Both men were plainly the worse for drink, and not only tipsy but also furiously angry. Oaths

The hawser was as taut as a bowstring

flew like hailstones, and every now and then there came forth such an explosion as I thought was sure to end in blows. But each time the quarrel passed off, and the voices grumbled lower for a while, until the next crisis came, and, in its turn, passed away without result.

On shore, I could see the glow of the great camp-fire burning warmly through the shore-side trees. Someone was singing, a dull, old, droning sailor's song, with a droop and a quaver at the end of every verse, and seemingly no end to it at all but the patience of the singer. I had heard it on the voyage more than once, and remembered these words:

> *But one man of her crew alive,*
> *What put to sea with seventy-five.*

I thought it was a ditty rather too dolefully appropriate for a company that had met such cruel losses in the morning. But, indeed, from what I saw, all these buccaneers were as callous as the sea they sailed on.

At last the breeze came; the schooner sidled and drew nearer in the dark; I felt the hawser slacken once more, and with a good, tough effort cut the last fibres through.

The breeze had but little action on the coracle, and I was almost instantly swept against the bows of the *Hispaniola*. At the same time the schooner began to turn upon her heel, spinning slowly, end for end, across the current.

I fought like a fiend, for I expected every moment to be swamped, and since I found I could not push the coracle directly off, I now shoved straight astern. At length I was clear of my dangerous neighbour and, just as I gave the last push, my hands came across a light cord that was trailing overboard across the stern bulwarks. Instantly I grasped it.

I pulled in hand over hand on the cord, rose to about half my height, and thus commanded the interior of the cabin. Hands and his companion were locked together in deadly wrestle, each with a hand upon the other's throat.

I dropped into the coracle again, none too soon, for I was near overboard. On the shore, the ballad had come to an end at last, and the whole diminished company about the camp-fire had broken into the chorus I had heard so often:

> *Fifteen men on the dead man's chest —*
> *Yo-ho-ho, and a bottle of rum!*
> *Drink and the devil had done for the rest —*
> *Yo-ho-ho, and a bottle of rum!*

Hands and his companion were locked together in deadly wrestle

Suddenly I was surprised by a sudden lurch of the coracle. At the same moment she turned sharply and seemed to change her course. The speed in the meantime had strangely increased.

I opened my eyes at once. All round me were little ripples, breaking over with a sharp, hissing sound and slightly phosphorescent. The *Hispaniola* herself, a few yards in whose wake I was still being whirled along, seemed to stagger in her course, and I saw her spars toss a little against the blackness of the night; nay, as I looked longer, I made sure she also was wheeling to the southward.

I glanced over my shoulder, and my heart jumped against my ribs. There, right behind me, was the glow of the camp-fire. The current had turned at right angles, sweeping round along with it the tall schooner and the little dancing coracle. Ever

[112]

quickening, ever bubbling higher, ever muttering louder, the waters went spinning through the narrows for the open sea.

Suddenly the schooner in front of me gave a violent lurch, turning, perhaps, through twenty degrees, and almost at the same moment one shout followed another from on board. I could hear feet pounding on the companion ladder, and I knew that the two drunkards had at last been interrupted in their quarrel and awakened to a sense of their disaster.

I lay down flat in the bottom of that wretched skiff, and devoutly recommended my spirit to its Maker.

So I must have lain for hours, continually beaten to and fro upon the billows, now and again wetted with flying spray, and never ceasing to expect death at the next plunge. Gradually weariness grew upon me; a numbness, an occasional stupor, fell upon my mind even in the midst of my terrors, until sleep came at last and in my sea-tossed coracle I lay and dreamed of home and the old 'Admiral Benbow'.

*   *   *   *   *

It was broad daylight when I awoke.

Haulbowline Head and Mizzen-mast Hill were at my elbow; the hill bare and dark, the head bounded by cliffs forty or fifty feet high, and fringed with great masses of fallen rock. I was scarce a quarter of a mile to seaward, and it was my first thought to paddle in and land.

That notion was soon given over. Among the fallen rocks the breakers spouted and bellowed; loud reverberations, heavy waves flying and falling, succeeded one another from second to second and I saw myself, if I ventured nearer, dashed to death

[113]

upon the rough shore, or spending my strength in vain scaling the beetling crags.

In the meantime I had a better chance, as I supposed, before me. North of Haulbowline Head, the land runs in a long way, leaving, at low tide, a long stretch of yellow sand. To the north of that, again, there comes another cape—Cape of the Woods, as it was marked upon the chart—buried in tall green pines, which descended to the margin of the sea.

I remembered what Silver had said about the current that set northward along the whole west coast of Treasure Island, and seeing from my position that I was already under its influence, I preferred to leave Haulbowline Head behind me, and reserve my strength for an attempt to land upon the kindlier-looking Cape of the Woods.

I began after a little to grow very bold, and sat up to try my skill at paddling. But even a small change in the disposition of the weight produced violent changes in the behaviour of the coracle. I had hardly moved before the boat, giving up at once her gentle dancing movement, ran straight down a slope of water so steep that it made me giddy, and struck her nose, with a spout of spray, deep into the side of the next wave.

I was drenched and terrified, and fell instantly back into my old position, whereupon the coracle seemed to find her head again, and led me as softly as before among the billows. It was plain she was not to be interfered with, and, at that rate, since I could in no way influence her course, what hope had I left of reaching land?

I began to be horribly frightened, but I kept my head for all that. First, moving with all care, I gradually baled out the coracle with my sea-cap. Then, getting my eye once more above

[114]

the gunwale, I set myself to study how it was she managed to slip so quietly through the rollers.

I found each wave, instead of the big, smooth, glossy mountain it looks from shore, or from a vessel's deck, was for all the world like any range of hills on the dry land, full of peaks and smooth places and valleys. The coracle, left to herself, turning from side to side, threaded, so to speak, her way through these lower parts, and avoided the steep slopes and higher, toppling summits of the wave.

'Well, now,' thought I to myself, 'it is plain I must lie where I am, and not disturb the balance; but it is plain, also, that I can put the paddle over the side, and from time to time, in smooth places, give her a shove or two towards land.' No sooner thought upon than done. There I lay on my elbows, in the most trying attitude, and every now and again gave a weak stroke or two to turn her head to shore.

It was very tiring, and slow work, yet I did visibly gain ground and as we drew near the Cape of the Woods, though I saw I must infallibly miss that point, I had still made some hundred yards of easting. I was, indeed, close in. I could see the cool, green tree-tops swaying together in the breeze, and I felt sure I should make the next promontory without fail.

It was high time, for I now began to be tortured with thirst, but as the next reach of sea opened out I beheld a sight that changed the nature of my thoughts.

Right in front of me, not half a mile away, I could see the *Hispaniola* under sail. I made sure, of course, that I should be taken, but I was so distressed for want of water, that I scarce knew whether to be glad or sorry. And, long before I had come to a conclusion, surprise had taken entire possession of my mind, and I could do nothing but stare and wonder.

The *Hispaniola* was under her mainsail and two jibs, and the beautiful white canvas shone in the sun like snow or silver. When I first sighted her, all her sails were drawing. She was lying a course about north-west, and I presumed the men on board were going round the island on their way back to the anchorage. Presently she began to fetch more and more to the westward, so that I thought they had sighted me and were going about in chase. At last, however, she fell right into the wind's eye, was taken dead aback, and stood there a while helpless, with her sails shivering.

'Clumsy fellows,' said I. 'They must still be drunk as owls.' And I thought how Captain Smollett would have set them skipping had he been on board.

Meanwhile the schooner gradually fell off, and filled again upon another tack, sailed swiftly for a minute or two, and brought up once more dead in the wind's eye. Again and again was this repeated. To and fro, up and down, north, south, east and west, the *Hispaniola* sailed by swoops, and dashes and at each repetition ended as she had begun, with idly flapping canvas. It became plain to me that nobody was steering. And, if so, where were the men? Either they were dead drunk, or had deserted her, I thought, and perhaps if I could get on board, I might return the vessel to her captain.

The current was bearing coracle and schooner southward at an equal rate. As for the latter's sailing, it was so wild and intermittent, and she hung each time so long in irons, that she certainly gained nothing, if she did not even lose. If only I dared to sit up and paddle, I made sure that I could overhaul her. The scheme had an air of adventure that inspired me, and the thought of the water beaker beside the fore companion doubled my growing courage.

Up I got, was welcomed almost instantly by another cloud of spray, but this time stuck to my purpose and set myself, with all my strength and caution, to paddle after the unsteered *Hispaniola*. Once I shipped a sea so heavy that I had to stop and bale, with my heart fluttering like a bird, but gradually I got into the way of the thing, and guided my coracle among the waves, with only now and then a blow upon her bows and a dash of foam in my face.

I was now gaining rapidly on the schooner. I could see the brass glisten on the tiller as it banged about, and still no soul appeared upon her decks. I could only suppose she was deserted. If not, the men were lying drunk below, where I might batten them down, perhaps, and do what I chose with the ship.

For some time she had been doing the very worst thing possible for me. She was headed nearly due south and thus it was difficult to gain on her, for helpless as she looked with the canvas cracking like cannon, and the blocks trundling and banging on the deck, she still continued to run away from me, not only with the speed of the current, but by the whole amount of her leeway, which was naturally great.

But now, at last, I had my chance. The breeze fell, for some seconds, very low, and the current gradually turning her, the *Hispaniola* revolved slowly round her centre, and at last presented me her stern, with the cabin window still gaping open, and the lamp over the table still burning on into the day. The mainsail hung, drooped like a banner. She was stock-still, but for the current.

For the last little while I had lost ground; but now redoubling my efforts, I began once more to overhaul the chase.

I was not a hundred yards from her when the wind came again in a clap. She filled on the port tack, and was off again, stooping and skimming like a swallow.

My first impulse was one of despair, but my second was towards joy. Round she came, till she was broadside on to me—round still till she had covered a half, and then two-thirds, and then three-quarters of the distance that separated us. I could see the waves boiling white under her forefoot. Immensely tall she looked to me from my low station in the coracle.

And then, of a sudden, I began to comprehend. I had scarce time to think—scarce time to act and save myself. I was on the summit of one swell when the schooner came swooping over the next. The bowsprit was over my head. I sprang to my feet, and leaped, stamping the coracle under water. With one hand I caught the jib-boom while my foot was wedged between the stay and the brace, and as I still clung there panting, a dull blow told me that the schooner had charged down upon and struck the coracle, and that I was left without retreat on the *Hispaniola*.

*   *   *   *   *

I had scarce gained a position on the bowsprit, when the flying jib flapped and filled upon the other tack, with a report like a gun. The schooner trembled to her keel under the reverse, but next moment, the other sails still drawing, the jib flapped back again, and hung idle.

This had nearly tossed me off into the sea, so now I lost

no time, crawled back along the bowsprit, and tumbled head foremost on the deck.

I was on the lee side of the forecastle, and the mainsail, which was still drawing, concealed from me a certain portion of the after-deck. Not a soul was to be seen. The planks, which had not been swabbed since the mutiny, bore the print of many feet, and an empty bottle, broken by the neck, tumbled to and fro like a live thing in the scuppers.

The jibs behind me cracked aloud; the rudder slammed to; the whole ship gave a sickening heave and shudder and at the same moment the main-boom swung inboard.

There were the two watchmen, sure enough; red-cap on his back, as stiff as a handspike, with his arms stretched out and his teeth showing through his open lips; Israel Hands propped against the bulwarks, his chin on his chest, his hands lying open before him on the deck, his face as white, under its tan, as a tallow candle. They had both evidently been dead some hours.

As the ship kept bucking and sidling like a vicious horse, the sails filling, now on one tack, now on another and the boom swinging to and fro, the dead men also slipped to and fro. Around both of them there were splashes of dark blood upon the planks, and it was obvious that they had killed each other in their drunken wrath.

I began to see a danger to the ship. The two jibs I speedily brought tumbling to the deck, but the mainsail was a harder matter. Of course, when the schooner tilted over, the boom had swung outboard, and the cap of it and a foot or two of sail hung even under water. I thought this made it still more dangerous, yet the strain was so heavy that I half feared to meddle. At last I got my knife and cut the halyards. The peak

I crawled back along the bowsprit

dropped instantly, a great belly of loose canvas floated broad upon the water and since, pull as I liked, I could not budge the downhaul, that was the extent of what I could accomplish. For the rest, the *Hispaniola* must trust to luck, like myself.

As the sun was setting she drove aground and began to settle on her beam-ends and I scrambled forward and looked over. It seemed shallow enough, and holding the cut hawser in both hands for a last security, I let myself drop softly overboard. The water scarcely reached my waist; the sand was firm and covered with ripple marks, and I waded ashore in great spirits, leaving the *Hispaniola* on her side, with her mainsail trailing wide upon the surface of the bay. About the same time the sun went fairly down and the breeze whistled low in the dusk among the tossing pines, and I recalled that I had been a whole night and a day at sea.

At last I was on land again, neither had I returned empty-handed. There lay the schooner, clear at last from buccaneers and ready for our own men to board and get to sea again. I had nothing nearer my fancy than to get home to the stockade and boast of my achievements. Possibly I might be blamed a bit for my truancy, but the recapture of the *Hispaniola* was a convincing answer, and I hoped that even Captain Smollett would confess that I had not wasted my time.

So thinking, and in famous spirits, I began to set my face homeward for the blockhouse and my companions. Although it was completely dark by the time I drew near to the stockade, I was surprised to find that I was allowed to climb the surrounding fence unchallenged.

They kept an infamous watch there. If it had been Silver and his lads that were now creeping in on them, not a soul would have seen daybreak.

I had crept cautiously to the door and stood up. All was dark within, so that I could distinguish nothing by eye.

With my arms before me, I walked steadily in. I should lie down in my own place (I thought, with a silent chuckle) and enjoy their faces when they found me in the morning.

My foot struck something yielding—it was a sleeper's leg, and he turned and groaned, but without awakening.

And then, all of a sudden, a shrill voice broke forth out of the darkness:

'Pieces of eight! Pieces of eight! Pieces of eight! Pieces of eight! Pieces of eight!' and so forth, without pause or change, like the clacking of a tiny mill.

Silver's green parrot, Captain Flint! It was she, keeping better watch than any human being, who thus announced my arrival with her wearisome refrain.

[121]

I let myself drop softly overboard

I had no time left to recover. At the sharp, clipping tone of the parrot, the sleepers awoke and sprang up, and with a mighty oath, the voice of Silver cried:

'Who goes?'

I turned to run, struck violently against one person, recoiled, and ran full into the arms of a second, who, for his part, closed upon and held me.

'Bring a torch, Dick,' said Silver, when my capture was thus assured.

And one of the men left the log-house and presently returned with a lighted brand from the fire which was kept burning in the compound.

The red glare of the torch, lighting up the interior of the blockhouse, showed me that the worst of my fears were realized. The pirates were in possession of the house and stores. There

'Who goes?'

was the cask of cognac, there were the pork and bread, as before, and what tenfold increased my horror, not a sign of any prisoner. I could only judge that all had perished, and my heart smote me sorely that I had not been there to perish with them.

There were six of the buccaneers all told; not another man was left alive.

The parrot sat, preening her plumage, on Long John's shoulder. He himself, I thought, looked somewhat paler and more stern than usual.

'So,' said he, 'here's Jim Hawkins, shiver my timbers! Dropped in, like, eh? Well, come, I take that friendly.'

And thereupon he sat down across the brandy cask and began to fill a pipe.

'Now, you see, Jim, so be as you *are* here,' said he, 'I'll give you a piece of my mind. You can't go back to your lot, for they won't have you, and without you start a third ship's company all by yourself, which might be lonely, you'll have to join with Cap'n Silver.'

'Well,' said I, growing a bit bolder, 'if I'm to choose, I declare that I have a right to know what's what, and why you're here and where my friends are.'

'Yesterday morning, Mr. Hawkins,' said he, 'in the dog-watch down came Dr. Livesey with a flag of truce. Says he, "Cap'n Silver, you're sold out. Ship's gone." Well, maybe we'd been taking a glass, and a song to help it round. I won't say no. Leastways none of us had looked. We looked out then, and, by thunder — the old ship *was* gone. I never seen a pack o' fools look sillier than we did.

"Well," says the doctor, "Let's bargain."

'We bargained, him and I, and here we are, stores, brandy, blockhouse. As for them, they've tramped; I don't know where's they are.'

'And now am I to choose?'

'And now you are to choose, and you may lay to that,' said Silver.

'Well,' said I, 'I am not such a fool but I know pretty well what I have to look for. Kill me, if you please, or spare me. But one thing I'll say, and no more; if you spare me, bygones are bygones, and when you fellows are in court for piracy, I'll save you all I can. It is for you to choose. Kill me and do yourselves no good, or spare me and keep a witness to save you from the gallows.'

For a moment not a man moved, but all sat staring at me like so many sheep.

'*I'll be hanged if I'll be bullied by you, John Silver*'

Then one of the pirates, old Tom Morgan sprang up, drawing his knife as if he had been twenty. 'Avast there,' cried Silver. Morgan paused, but a hoarse murmur rose from the others. 'Tom's right,' said one.

'I stood bullying long enough from one,' added another. 'I'll be hanged if I'll be bullied by you, John Silver.'

'Did any of you gentlemen want to have it out with *me*?' roared Silver, bending far forward from his position on the keg, with his pipe still glowing in his right hand. 'Kill that boy? Not me, mates! Why, shiver my timbers! Isn't he a hostage? Are we going to waste a hostage? No, not us, he might be our last chance to make a bargain with.'

'Bargains!' Morgan growled. 'Why d'ye make these bargains, John?'

'Why, you'd have starved if I hadn't—but that's a trifle! You look there—that's why!'

And he cast down upon the floor a paper that I instantly recognized. None other than the chart on yellow paper, with the three red crosses, that I had found in the oilskin at the bottom of the captain's chest. Why the doctor had given it to him was more than I could fancy, but it served to turn the men's ugly mood, and as they passed it from hand to hand in high good humour, Silver drew me aside.

'Now, look you here, Jim Hawkins, you're within half a plank of death, or torture, which is worse. They're going to throw me off, but, you mark, I'll stand by you through thick and thin. I'll save your life — if so be I can — from them. But, see here, Jim — tit for tat — you save Long John from swinging.'

I was bewildered; it seemed a hopeless thing he was asking.

'What I can do, that I'll do,' I said.

'It's a bargain!' cried Long John. 'Understand me Jim, I've a head on my shoulders, I have. I'm on squire's side now. I know you've got that ship safe somewheres. How you done it I don't know, but safe I believe it is.' He took a swallow of brandy as the men rejoined us, and took command, posting one man as a sentry and telling the others, including myself, to get some sleep before day. In spite of being desperately tired, I found it impossible to sleep straight away. My poor head was in a whirl. What had happened to my friends? Why had they apparently surrendered their little stronghold, their stores, and most amazing of all, the precious map? Undoubtedly Captain Smollett would consider my seeming desertion a breach of discipline, but I had hoped that my action in capturing the *Hispaniola* would compensate for this defection. At last,

I had a line about my waist, and followed obediently after the sea cook

I fell into a troubled, uneasy sleep, wondering what the morning would bring to my unenviable position.

* * * * *

At full daylight we all had a rough breakfast, and then set out to dig for the treasure. We made a curious sight, had anyone been there to see us, all in soiled sailor clothes, and all but me armed to the teeth. Silver had two guns slung about him—one before and one behind—besides the great cutlass at his waist, and a pistol in each pocket of his square-tailed coat. To complete his strange appearance, Captain Flint sat perched upon his shoulder and gabbled odds and ends of sea-talk. I had a line about my waist, and followed obediently after the sea cook, who held the loose end of the rope, now in his free hand, now between his powerful teeth. For all the world, I was led like a dancing bear.

The cache had been found and rifled

We all set out, the party spreading itself abroad in a fan shape, shouting and leaping to and fro. About the centre, and a good way behind the rest, Silver and I followed—I tethered to my rope, he ploughing with deep pants along the sliding gravel. As we made our way over the rough ground, there was some discussion about the chart. The red cross was far too large to be a guide, and each man had a different idea as to which was the tall tree referred to in the notes written on the back.

As we approached the brow of the plateau we felt obliged to sit down and rest for a few minutes. All of a sudden, out of the middle of the trees in front of us, a thin, high, trembling voice struck up the well-known air and words:

> *Fifteen men on the dead man's chest—*
> *Yo-ho-ho, and a bottle of rum!*

[128]

I have never seen men more dreadfully affected than the pirates. The colour went from their six faces like enchantment. Some leapt to their feet, some clawed hold of others, and Morgan grovelled on the ground.

'It's Flint, by——!'

The song had stopped as suddenly as it began—broken off, you would have said, in the middle of a note as though someone had laid his hand upon the singer's mouth.

'Come,' said Silver, struggling with his ashen lips to get the word out, 'this won't do. Stand by to go about. This is a rum start, and I can't name the voice; but it's someone skylarking—someone that's flesh and blood, and you may lay to that.'

His courage had come back as he spoke, and some of the colour to his face along with in. Already the others had begun to lend an ear to this encouragement, and were coming a little to themselves, when the same voice broke out again in a faint distant hail, that echoed among the clefts of the Spy-glass.

'Darby M'Graw,' it wailed—for that is the word that best describes the sound—'Darby M'Graw! Darby M' Graw!' again and again and again; and then rising a little higher, and with an oath that I leave out, 'Fetch aft the rum, Darby!'

The buccaneers remained rooted to the ground, their eyes starting from their heads. Long after the voice had died away they still stared in silence, dreadfully, before them.

'That fixes it,' said one. 'Let's go!'

'They was Flint's last words,' moaned Morgan, 'his last words above board.'

Still, Silver was unconquered. I could hear his teeth rattle in his head; but he had not yet surrendered.

[129]

'By the powers, Ben Gunn!' he roared suddenly.

'Aye, and so it were,' cried Morgan, 'Ben Gunn it were!'

It was extraordinary how their spirits had returned and how the natural colour had revived in their faces. Soon they were chatting together, and not long after, hearing no further sound, they shouldered the tools and set forth again.

We arrived at the margin of the thicket.

'Huzza, mates, all together!' shouted Morgan, and the foremost broke into a run.

And suddenly, not ten yards farther, Silver and I saw them stop. A low cry arose. Silver doubled his pace, digging away with the foot of his crutch like one possessed; and the next moment he and I had come also to a dead halt.

Before us was a great excavation, not very recent, for the sides had fallen in and grass had sprouted on the bottom. In this was the shaft of a pick broken in two with the boards of several packing-cases strewn around. On one of these boards I saw, branded with a hot iron, the name *Walrus*—the name of Flint's ship.

All was clear as daylight. The *cache* had been found and rifled and the seven hundred thousand pounds were gone!

There was never such an overturn in this world. Each of these six men was as though he had been struck, but with Silver the blow passed almost instantly. Every thought of his soul had been set full-stretch, like a racer, on that money. Well, he was brought up in a single second, dead, but he kept his head, found his temper, and changed his plan before the others had had time to realize the disappointment.

'Jim,' he whispered, 'take that and stand by for trouble.'

And he passed me a double-barrelled pistol.

The buccaneers, with oaths and cries, began to leap, one after another, into the pit and to dig with their fingers, throwing the boards aside as they did so. Morgan found a piece of gold. He held it up with a perfect spout of oaths. It was a two-guinea piece and it went from hand to hand among them for a quarter of a minute.

'Two guineas!' roared Morgan, shaking it at Silver. 'That's your seven hundred thousand pounds, is it? You're the man for bargains, ain't you?'

But this time everyone was entirely in Morgan's favour. They began to scramble out of the excavation, darting furious glances behind them.

Well, there we stood, two on one side, five on the other, the pit between us, and nobody screwed up high enough to offer the first blow. Silver never moved; he watched them, very upright on his crutch, and looked as cool as ever.

'Mates,' says Morgan, 'there's two of them alone there. One's the old cripple that brought us all here and blundered us down to this; the other's that cub that I mean to have the heart of. Now, mates——'

He was raising his arm and his voice, and plainly meant to lead a charge. But just then — crack! crack! crack! — three musket-shots flashed out of the thicket. Morgan tumbled head foremost into the excavation; the man with the bandage spun round like a top, and fell all his length upon his side, where he lay dead, but still twitching; and the other three turned and ran for it with all their might.

Before you could wink, Long John had fired two barrels of

a pistol into the struggling Morgan; and as the man rolled up his eyes at him in the last agony, 'Tom,' said he, 'I reckon I settled you.'

At the same moment the doctor, Gray, and Ben Gunn joined us, with smoking muskets, from among the nutmeg trees.

'Thank you kindly,' said Silver. 'You came in about the nick, I guess, for me and Hawkins. So it's you, Ben Gunn!' he added. 'Well, you're a nice one to be sure.'

'I'm Ben Gunn, I am,' replied the maroon, wriggling like an eel in his embarrassment. 'And,' he added, after a long pause, 'how do, Mr. Silver? Pretty well, I thank ye, says you.'

'Ben, Ben,' murmured Silver, 'to think as you've done me!'

The doctor sent back Gray for one of the pickaxes, deserted by the mutineers in their flight; and then, as we proceeded slowly downhill to Ben's Cave, related in a few words what had taken place and this story answered all the questions which had been going round and round in my head. It was a story that profoundly interested Silver; and Ben Gunn, the half-idiot maroon, was the hero from the beginning.

Ben, in his long, lonely wanderings about the island, had found the treasure; he had dug it up, carried it on his back to a cave he had on the two-pointed hill at the north-east angle of the island, and there it had lain in safety since two months before the arrival of the *Hispaniola*.

When the doctor had wormed this secret from him, on the afternoon of the attack, and when next morning, he saw the anchorage deserted, he had gone to Silver, given him the chart, which was now useless—given him the stores, for Ben Gunn's cave was well supplied with goats' meat salted by himself—given anything and everything to get a chance of moving in safety from the stockade to the two-pointed hill, there to be clear of malaria and to keep a guard on the money.

As we passed the two-pointed hill we could see the black mouth of Ben Gunn's cave, and a figure standing by it, leaning on a musket. It was Squire Trelawny, and we waved a handkerchief and gave him three cheers, in which the voice of Silver joined as heartily as any. At Silver's polite salute the squire flushed somewhat.

'John Silver,' he said, 'You're a prodigious villain and impostor—a monstrous impostor, sir.' In a few words, I whispered to the squire of my pact with Silver, and told how he had saved me from the men the previous night. He looked at Silver again severely. 'I am told I am not to prosecute you. Well, then I will not. But the dead men, sir, hang about your head like millstones.'

'Thank you kindly, sir,' replied Long John, again saluting.

'I dare you to thank me!' cried the squire. 'It is a gross dereliction of my duty. Stand back.'

And thereupon we all entered the cave. It was a large, airy place, with a little spring and a pool of clear water, overhung with ferns. The floor was sand. Before a big fire lay Captain Smollett, and in a far corner, only duskily flickered over by the blaze, I beheld great heaps of coin and bars of gold. That was Flint's treasure that we had come so far to seek, and that had cost already the lives of seventeen men from the *Hispaniola*.

'Come in, Jim,' said the Captain. 'You're a good boy in your line, Jim; but I don't think you and me'll go to sea again. You're too much of the born favourite for me. Is that you, John Silver? What brings you here, man?'

'Come back on my dooty, sir,' returned John.

[133]

'Ah!' said the captain, and that was all he said.

Well, to make a long story short, we got a few hands on board, made a good cruise home. On the homeward journey, while we were calling at a South American port for supplies, Silver escaped from the ship, stealing one of the sacks of coin, but I think we were all glad to be so cheaply quit of him. The *Hispaniola* reached Bristol just as Mr. Blandy was beginning to think of fitting out her consort to come and search for us. Five men only of those who had sailed returned with her. 'Drink and the devil had done for the rest' with a vengeance; although, to be sure we were not in quite as bad a case as the other ship they sang about:

> *With one man of her crew alive,*
> *What put to sea with seventy-five.*

All of us had an ample share of the treasure, and used it wisely or foolishly, according to our natures.

The bar silver and arms still lie, for all that I know, where Flint buried them; and certainly they shall still lie there for me. Oxen and wain-ropes would not bring me again to that accursed island; and the worst dreams I have are when I hear the surf booming about its coasts, or start upright in bed with the sharp voice of Captain Flint, Silver's parrot, still ringing in my ears: 'Pieces of eight! Pieces of eight!'

KIDNAPPED

by

ROBERT LOUIS STEVENSON

I will begin the story of my adventures with a certain morning early in the month of June, the year of grace 1751, when I took the key for the last time out of the door of my father's house.

Mr Campbell, the minister of Essendean, was waiting for me by the garden gate, good man!

'Well Davie, lad,' said he, 'I will go with you so far as the ford, to set you on your way.'

And we began to walk forward in silence.

'Are ye sorry to leave Essendean?' said he, after a while.

'Why, sir,' said I, 'if I knew where I was going, or what was likely to become of me, I would tell you. Essendean is a good place indeed, and I have been very happy there, but then I have never been anywhere else. My father and mother, since they are both dead, I shall be no nearer to in Essendean than in the Kingdom of Hungary. And, to speak truth, if I thought

I had a chance to better myself where I was going I would go with a good will.'

'Ay?' said Mr Campbell. 'Very well, Davie. Then I must tell you your fortune, or so far as I may. When your mother was gone, and your father was taken ill before he died, he gave me a certain letter. "As soon," says he, "as I am gone, give my boy this letter into his hand, and start him off to the house of Shaws, not far from Cramond." '

'The house of Shaws!' I cried. 'What had my poor father to do with the house of Shaws?'

'Well,' said Mr Campbell, 'who can tell for certain? But the name of that family, Davie boy, is the name you bear —Balfour of Shaws. Here is the name, written on the letter itself by your father.'

He gave me the letter, which was addressed in these words: 'To the hands of Ebenezer Balfour, Esq., of Shaws, in his house of Shaws, these will be delivered by my son, David Balfour.' My heart was beating hard at this great prospect now suddenly opening before a lad of seventeen years of age, the son of a poor country schoolmaster in the Forest of Ettrick.

Two days of eager walking brought me to Cramond and I sat me down and stared at the house of Shaws. The more I looked, the pleasanter that countryside appeared, yet the house in the midst of it was not much to my liking. The nearer I got to it, the drearier it appeared. It seemed like part of a house that had never been finished. What should have been one end stood open on the upper floors, and one could see against the sky steps and stairs which were not finished. Many of the windows had no glass and bats flew in and out like doves out of a dovecote.

Bats flew in and out like doves out of a dovecote

The night had begun to fall as I got close, and in three of the lower windows, which were very high up and narrow and well barred, the changing light of a little fire began to glimmer.

Was this the place I had been coming to? Was it within these walls that I was to seek new friends and begin great fortunes?

I came forward cautiously, and listening as I came, heard someone rattling with dishes, and now and again a little dry, quick cough, but there was no sound of speech and not a dog barked.

The door, as well as I could see it in the dim light, was a great piece of wood all covered with nails, and I lifted my hand and knocked once. Then I stood and waited. The house had fallen into a dead silence; I knocked again, and listened again. By this time my ears had grown so used to the quiet, that I could hear the ticking of the clock inside as it slowly counted out the seconds, but whoever was in the house kept deadly still, and must have held his breath.

Then I got angry. I began to kick and bang on the door, and to shout out aloud for Mr Balfour. I was still kicking away when I heard the cough right overhead, and jumping back and looking, saw a man's head in a tall nightcap, and the end of a blunderbuss pointing at me, at one of the upper windows.

'It's loaded,' said a voice.

'I have come here with a letter,' I said, 'to Mr Ebenezer Balfour of Shaws. Is he here?'

'What?' cried the voice sharply.

I repeated what I had said.

'Who are ye, yourself?' was the next question, after a long pause.

'I am not ashamed of my name,' said I. 'They call me David Balfour.'

At that, I made sure the man started, for I heard the blunderbuss rattle on the window sill, and it was after quite a long pause, and with a curious change of voice, that the next question followed:

'Is your father dead?'

I was so much surprised at this that I could find no voice to answer, but stood staring.

'Ay,' the man resumed, 'he'll be dead, no doubt, and that'll be what brings ye to my door.' Another pause, and then defiantly. 'Well, man,' he said, 'I'll let ye in,' and he disappeared from the window.

★ ★ ★ ★ ★

*. . . a man's head in a tall nightcap and the end of a blunderbuss
pointing at me . . .*

Presently there came a great rattling of chains and bolts, and
the door was cautiously opened and shut again behind me as
soon as I had passed.

As soon as the last chain was up, the man looked at me.
He was a small, bent, narrow-shouldered, pale-faced creature,
and his age might have been anything between fifty and seventy.
His nightcap was of flannel, and so was the nightgown that
he wore, instead of coat and waistcoat, over his ragged shirt.
He was long unshaved, but what most distressed and even
daunted me, was that he would neither take his eyes away
from me nor look me fairly in the face. What he was, whether
by trade or birth, was more than I could guess, but he seemed

very like an old servant, who might have been left to look after that big house for wages.

'Let's see the letter,' said he.

I told him the letter was for Mr Balfour, not for him.

'And who do ye think I am?' says he. 'Give me Alexanders' letter.'

'You know my father's name?'

'I'm your uncle, Davie, my man, and you're my nephew. So give us the letter, and sit down.'

If I had been some years younger, what with shame, weariness, and dispointment, I believe I would have burst into tears. As it was, I could find no words, but handed him the letter and sat down.

My uncle, stooping over the fire, turned the letter over and over in his hand.

'Your father's long been dead?' he asked.

'Three weeks, sir,' said I.

'He was a secret man, Alexander—a secret, silent man,' he continued. 'Did he ever speak of me?'

'I never knew, sir, till you told me yourself, that he had any brother.'

'Dear me, dear me!' said Ebenezer. 'You have not heard of Shaws, I dare say?'

'Not till I was given that letter, sir,' said I.

'To think of that!' said he. 'A strange man!' For all that, he seemed satisfied, but whether with himself, or me, or with this conduct of my father's, was more than I could understand. Certainly, however, he seemed to be getting over his first dislike of me, for he presently jumped up, came across the room behind me, and hit me smack upon the shoulder. 'We'll agree

He turned the letter over and over in his hand

fine yet!' he cried. 'I'm just as glad I let you in. And now come to your bed.'

As soon as day broke I opened my eyes to find myself in a great room, furnished with fine furniture, and lit by three big windows. Ten years ago, or perhaps twenty, it must have been as pleasant a room to lie down or awake in as a man could wish, but damp, dirt, disuse, mice, and spiders had done their worst since then.

My uncle took me to the back of the house, where there was a well, and told me to 'wash my face there, if I wanted'; and when that was done I made the best of my own way back to the kitchen, where he had lit the fire and was making porridge.

When we had made an end of our meal, my uncle Ebenezer

unlocked a drawer, and drew out of it a clay pipe and a lump of tobacco, from which he cut a piece before he locked it up again. Then he sat down in the sun at one of the windows and silently smoked.

'Davie, my boy,' said he at last, 'ye've come to the right place when ye came to your Uncle Ebenezer. I'm very fond of my family, and I mean to do right by you. Stay here quiet a while, and ye'll find that we get on.'

'Well, sir,' said I, after I had thought the matter out in silence, 'I'll stay a while. It's more just I should be helped by my own relations than strangers, and if we don't agree — I'll do my best — it shall be through no fault of mine.'

The day passed fairly well. We had the porridge cold again at noon, and hot porridge at night; porridge and beer was my uncle's diet. He spoke but little, occasionally questioning me after a long silence, but when I sought to talk about my future, he fell silent.

One thing I discovered which put me in some doubt. This was an entry on the flyleaf of a book plainly written by my father's hand: 'To my brother Ebenezer on his fifth birthday.' Now what puzzled me was this: that as my father was of course the younger brother, he must either have made some strange error, or he must have written, before he was yet five, excellent, clear, grown-up writing.

When at length I went back to the kitchen, and sat down, the first thing I said to Uncle Ebenezer was to ask him if my father had not been very quick at school.

'Alexander? Not him!' was the reply. 'I was far quicker myself. I was a clever chappie when I was young. Why, I could read as soon as he could.'

My uncle had cleared the table and now sat smoking a pipe

This puzzled me yet more, and a thought coming into my head, I asked if he and my father had been twins.

He jumped upon his stool, and the spoon fell out of his hand upon the floor. 'Why do you ask that?' he said, and he caught me by the jacket, looking this time straight into my eyes. His own were little and light and bright like a bird's.

'What do you mean?' I asked, very calmly, for I was far stronger than he, and not easily frightened. 'Take your hand from my jacket. This is no way to behave.'

My uncle seemed to make a great effort, and then in a queer voice, said, 'You shouldn't speak to me about your father. That's what upsets me.' Then he added, 'He was my only brother,' but although he tried to make his voice sound sad, it did not ring true.

I began to wonder what was wrong with my uncle. And I thought of a song I knew which told how a wicked uncle kept a poor lad from claiming a fortune which really belonged to him. Could it be that my uncle was trying to stop me getting some fortune that belonged to *me*?

My uncle had cleared the table and now sat smoking a pipe.

After some time, 'Davie,' he said, 'there's a little money which I promised to give to you one day. I promised your father before you were born. It's forty pounds.' He said this as though he did not like saying it.

I was sure that he was telling me a lie but I could not guess why he had made the offer.

However I had no reason not to take the money and he counted me out forty pounds, after he had asked me to step outside for a minute so that I could not see where he had got it from.

'There,' he said, as he gave it to me, 'that's to prove that I do my duty. Not everyone would have done it. But it's a pleasure to do right by my brother's son and it's a pleasure to think that we can now be friends.'

I thanked him, but still wondered what he was up to. Then I offered to give him some help about the house in return for his gift.

'Well,' he said, 'let's begin now.' He pulled from his pocket a rusty key to the stair tower at the end of the house. 'You can only get into it from the outside, for that part of the house is not finished. Go in and up the stairs and bring me down the chest at the top. There are papers in it,' he added.

'Can I have a light?' I said.

'No,' he said, 'no lights in my house!'

[145]

I went forward very slowly on my hands and knees

'Very well, sir,' I said, 'are the stairs good?'

'Fine!' he answered, then added, 'keep to the wall, for there are no banisters.'

Out I went into the night. It was very black and though the wind moaned in the distance it was quite still around the house. I felt my way along the wall until I came to the unfinished part of the house. I was just unlocking the door when a sudden flash of lightning lit up the sky. For a moment I could hardly see and was half blind as I stepped into the tower. I groped my way forward and soon found the lowest step of the stairs and the opposite wall of the tower.

The steps seemed solid and firm enough and I went steadily up them for four floors, keeping well against the wall.

Suddenly there was another flash of lightning and I was

[146]

seized with fear. My foot was only two inches from the edge of the stairs and there was a sheer drop to the ground far below, with nothing to stop me falling over on that side.

Then I became very angry. It was very dangerous for my uncle to have sent me climbing up these stairs. But I decided that I would still go on up to look in the chest. I went forward very slowly on my hands and knees feeling each step before me as I went and then I suddenly felt nothing in front and a flash of lightning showed—that the steps ended in mid-air. My heart almost stopped beating. My uncle had tried to kill me—; that was certain.

As I went slowly down, heavy rain began to fall and the wind began to howl. When I got out of the tower there was another bright flash of lightning followed immediately by a great crash of thunder. The lightning showed up my uncle standing by the door of the kitchen looking up. At the crash of the thunder he seemed suddenly afraid and ran inside banging the door after him.

I ran across to the door and opened it. My uncle was inside with his back to me.

I stepped forward and suddenly clapped my hands on his shoulders. 'Ah!' I cried.

My uncle gave a cry like a sheep's bleat, threw up his arms and fell to the floor like a dead man.

After a few moments he opened his eyes and looked at me in terror.

'Are you alive?' he asked in a terrified voice.

'I am,' said I, 'but I have not got you to thank for it.'

He did not reply but seemed to be very tired and not able to speak.

I went to open the door and found a half-grown boy in seaclothes

I felt sorry for him, but remembering what he had done, I was very angry. Then I asked him why he had lied to me, why he had been so upset when I had asked if my father and he were twins, and lastly why he had tried to kill me.

He heard me without speaking. Then he begged me to let him go to bed.

'I'll tell you in the morning, as sure as anything, I will,' he said.

I locked him in his room and pocketed the key. Then, going back to the kitchen, I made up the fire and wrapping myself up in some blankets, I fell asleep.

* * * * *

[148]

Much rain fell in the night, and the next morning there was a bitter wind and lots of clouds. Soon we were having breakfast, just like the day before.

'Well, sir,' said I, 'have you nothing more to say to me?'

He murmured something and I saw by his face that though he had no lie ready for me, he was hard at work making one up. I think I was about to tell him so when we were interrupted by a knocking at the door.

Telling my uncle to sit where he was, I went to open it and found a half-grown boy, in seaman's clothes.

'Hallo, mate!' said he, with a cracked voice.

I asked him quietly what he wanted. He did not answer but began to sing.

'Well,' said I, 'if you do not want anything at all, I will even be so rude as to shut you out.'

'Wait, brother!' he cried. 'Have you no fun about you or do you want to get me into trouble? I've brought a letter from old Heasy-oasy to Mr Belflower.' He showed me a letter as he spoke. 'And I say, mate,' he added, 'I'm very hungry.'

'Well,' said I, 'come into the house, and you shall have a little to eat even if I go hungry.'

With that I brought him in and put him in my own place, where he greedily ate up the remains of breakfast. Meanwhile, my uncle had read the letter and sat thinking. Then, suddenly, he got to his feet quickly, and took me into the farthest corner of the room.

'Read that,' said he, and put the letter into my hand.

Here it is, lying before me as I write:

'The Hawes Inn, at the Queen's Ferry.

'Sir — I am staying here and my ship is ready to sail. If you have any further orders for overseas, to-day will be the last day, as the wind is a good one for sailing. I have had arguments with your agent, Mr Rankeillor; if things are not cleared up there will be trouble.

'Elias Hoseason.'

'You see, Davie,' my uncle went on as soon as I had read the letter, 'I do business with this man Hoseason, the captain of a ship, the *Covenant*. Now if you and I were to walk over with this lad, I could see the captain at the Hawes Inn, or maybe on board the *Covenant*.'

I stood awhile and thought. I was going to the town anyway. Once there, I believed I could force my uncle to visit the lawyer, so that I could find out what he was hiding from me, and I also really wished to see the sea and ships.

'Very well,' says I, 'let us go.'

My uncle got into his hat and coat, and then we put the fire out, locked the door, and set forth upon our walk.

As soon as we came to the inn, my uncle told me to wait.

The next thing, I heard my uncle calling me, and found him with the captain. It was the captain who spoke to me.

'Sir,' said he, 'Mr Balfour tells me great things of you, and for my part, I like your looks. I wish I was going to stay longer here, so that we might make the better friends, but we'll try to be friends as best we can. Ye shall come on board my ship for half an hour, till the tide begins to go out and have a drink with me.'

Now I longed to see the inside of a ship more than words

We set forth upon our walk

can tell, but I was not going to put myself in danger, and I told him my uncle and I were going to see a lawyer.

'Ay, ay,' said he, 'he told me about that.' And here he suddenly leaned down and whispered in my ear: 'Watch out for the old man; he means mischief. Come aboard till I can get a word with ye.' And then, passing his arm through mine, he set off towards his boat.

As soon as we were by the boat, Hoseason, saying that we must waste no time, ordered me to be pulled up over the side of the ship. I was quickly on deck, where the captain stood waiting for me, and slipped his arm under mine.

'But where is my uncle?' said I.

'Never mind,' said Hoseason, grabbing me suddenly.

I felt I was lost. With all my strength I got away from him, and ran to the side of the ship. Sure enough, there was the boat going back to the shore, with my uncle sitting in it. I gave a loud cry—'Help, help! Murder!'—and my uncle turned round where he was sitting, and showed me a face full of cruelty and terror.

It was the last I saw. Already strong hands had grabbed me and pulled me back from the ship's side, and then I saw a great flash of fire and fell senseless.

★ ★ ★ ★ ★

When I woke up I was in darkness, in great pain and deafened by many unfamiliar noises. I could hear the loud noise of water rushing, the sound of the sails flapping, and the shrill cries of seamen. The whole world now heaved giddily up, and now rushed giddily downward, and so sick and hurt was I in body, and my mind was so much upset, that it took me a long while trying to think where I was before I realised that I must be lying somewhere bound in Captain Hoseason's ship, and that there was a big storm.

I do not know how long I was lying there, but it seemed a very long time and I kept on expecting the ship to hit a rock, or to sink into the depths of the sea.

One night, about eleven o'clock, Captain Hoseason came down the ladder. He looked sharply round, and then, walking straight up to me, he spoke to me, to my surprise, in a kind voice.

'My boy,' said he, 'we want ye to wait at table. Off you go.'

The place where I was now to sleep and serve stood some

It took me a long while trying to think where I was

six feet above the crew decks, and, considering the size of the ship, was very big. Inside were a table, and bench fixed to the floor, and two rooms, one for the captain and the other for the two mates, who used it in turns. It was all fitted with cupboards from top to bottom, so that the officers' things and the ship's stores could be kept there. Indeed, all the best of the meat and drink and the whole of the gunpowder were collected in this place, and all the guns, except two brass ones, were put in a rack on the wall. Most of the swords were in another place, though there was another rack with some in it.

That was the first night of my new job, and during the next day I soon got to know what to do. I had to serve at the meals, which the captain took always at the proper time, sitting down with the officer who was off duty. All the day through I would be running about carrying something to one or the other of my three masters, and at night I slept on a blanket thrown on the floor at the back of the place, where it was very cold and the wind blew through the doors. I was very uncomfortable and I do not know how I survived.

* * * * *

More than a week went by in which the *Covenant* still did not get far on its voyage. Some days the ship did not go more than a mile or two; on other days she was actually driven back.

About ten o'clock one night I was serving the second mate, Mr Riach, and the captain at their supper when the ship struck something with a great sound, and we heard voices crying out. My two masters leapt to their feet.

We had run into a boat in the fog, and she had been cut in half and gone to the bottom with all her crew but one. This man had been brought in and when he took off his coat, he laid two beautiful silver pistols on the table, and I saw that he had on a great sword. He was very polite, but I thought even at the first sight, that here was a man I would rather call my friend than my enemy.

The captain, too, was looking at him, but mostly at the man's clothes. And to be sure, he was dressed very finely, having a hat with feathers, a red waistcoat, black breeches, and a blue coat with silver buttons and silver lace—costly clothes, though somewhat dirty from the fog and from being slept in.

And then, unhappily, the captain saw me standing in my

corner, and sent me off to the galley to get supper for the gentleman. I lost no time, I promise you, and when I came back, I found the gentleman had taken a belt with money in it from about his waist, and had put a gold coin or two upon the table. The captain was looking at the gold coins, and then at the belt, and then at the gentleman's face, and then at the belt again; and I thought he seemed excited.

'Half of it,' he cried, 'and I'm your man!'

The other put back the coins into the belt, and put it on again under his waistcoat. 'I have told ye, sir,' said he, 'that not one coin of it belongs to me. It belongs to my chieftain,' and here he touched his hat—'but I must get to shore safe and I will give you thirty gold coins if you will put me on the shore and sixty if you can get me to the Loch.'

'Well,' answered the captain, 'I agree; sixty gold coins!'

Then they shook hands.

And then the captain went out (rather hurriedly, I thought,) and left me alone with the stranger. I realised that this man was in the service of King Louis of France and Prince Charles, who wanted to be King of Scotland, and that he was probably going to Scotland to get money for Prince Charles from the followers of Charles there. Although I was on the opposite side, I could not look at such a man without a lively interest.

'And so you're in the service of Prince Charles,' said I, as I set a meal before him.

'Ay,' said he, beginning to eat; 'and I'm very thirsty. It's hard if I'm going to pay sixty gold coins and not get even a little to drink.'

'I'll go on deck and ask for the key,' said I, and left.

The fog was still thick, but the sea was calm. Some of the

[155]

He laid two beautiful silver pistols on the table

sailors were looking out for the shore, but the captain and the two officers were talking together. I thought (I don't know why) that they were up to no good, and the first word I heard, as I softly drew near, made me sure.

Mr Riach was saying, as if he had only just thought of it:

'Couldn't we get him out of the cabin?'

'He's better where he is,' answered Hoseason; 'he hasn't room to use his sword.'

'Well, that's true,' said Riach; 'but he's hard to get at.'

'Nonsense!' said Hoseason. 'We can get the man talking, one upon each side, and pin him by the two arms before he has time to get his sword out.'

On hearing this I was very afraid and angry at these wicked, greedy men that I sailed with. I hurried back to the cabin, where the man was still eating his supper under the lamp. I walked right up to the table and put my hand on his shoulder.

'Do you want to be killed?' said I.

He sprang to his feet and looked at me.

'Oh!' cried I, 'they're all murderers here. It's a ship full of them!'

'Ay, ay,' said he. And then, looking at me curiously, 'Will ye fight with me?'

'That will I!' said I. 'I am no thief, nor yet murderer. I'll stand by you.'

'Why, then,' said he, 'what's your name?'

'David Balfour,' said I, and thinking that a man with so fine a coat must like fine people, I added for the first time, 'of Shaws.'

'My name is Alan Breck,' he said, proudly, 'and I am in the service of Prince Charles.'

Then he at once began to look around to see how we could defend the cabin, which stood on the deck.

The cabin was built very strong, so that it would not be damaged by the waves. Only the window in the roof and the doors were large enough for a man to get through. The doors could be shut close. I was going to shut them when Alan stopped me.

'It would be better shut,' said I.

'Not so, David,' says he. 'Ye see, I have but one face, but so long as that door is open and my face to it, most of my enemies will be in front of me, where I would prefer to find them.'

Then he gave me from the rack a sword, choosing it with

I walked right up to the table, and put my hand on his shoulder

great care, shaking his head and saying he had never in all his life seen poorer weapons, and next he set me down at the table with some gunpowder, some bullets, and all the pistols, which he told me to load.

Then he stood up and faced the door, and drew his great sword. 'Now,' he said, 'keep loading the pistols when they are needed and obey my orders.'

* * * * *

We did not have to wait long. Just at this moment the captain appeared at the open door.

'Keep back!' cried Alan, and pointed his sword at him.

[158]

The captain stopped, but did not seem afraid.

'What are you doing with a sword?' said he. 'I thought we were friends.'

'No, you're not,' said Alan. 'You were planning to murder me. But I am not afraid. I am ready to fight, so if you want to begin I am ready for you and your wicked crew,' and he waved his sword.

The captain said nothing to Alan, but he looked over at me with an ugly look. Next moment he was gone.

'And now,' said Alan, 'get ready, David, for the fight will soon start.'

Suddenly a lot of the sailors rushed at the door with swords in their hands, and at the same moment, the glass of the window in the roof was broken in a thousand pieces, and a man jumped through and landed on the floor. Before he got to his feet, I gave a shout and shot him dead with one of the pistols. A second fellow then tried to jump down through the window but before he could I snatched another pistol and shot this one, so that he fell down with a bump on to the floor below. I did not have time to think, but just kept on grabbing pistol sand firing as fast as I could. For the moment no one else came through the roof window.

Then I heard Alan shout for help, and I turned round.

He had held the sailors back at the door but was finding it hard to keep them out now. There were many of them all trying to break through and one was just attacking Alan with his sword raised.

I thought he would certainly kill Alan so, grasping a sword, I attacked them from the side. But I had no time to be of help. Alan jumped back to get out of the way and give himself room

[159]

Just at this moment, the captain appeared at the door

and then rushed forward like a bull, shouting as he ran. All the sailors suddenly turned and fled, bumping into one another in their hurry.

We heard them tumble down a stairway and shut the door after them with a bang.

The cabin was in a mess; there were four men dead and there were Alan and I, victorious and unhurt.

He came up to me with open arms. 'Come to my arms!' he cried, and embraced me and kissed me hard upon both cheeks. 'David,' said he, 'I love you like a brother. And oh, man,' he cried happily, 'am I not a great fighter?'

But there was a tightness on my chest that I could hardly breathe. The thought of the two men I had shot was like a nightmare, and all of a sudden, and before I had a guess at what was following, I began to sob and cry like any child.

Alan put his hand on my shoulder, and said I was a brave lad and wanted nothing but sleep.

'I'll take the first turn at keeping watch,' said he. 'You've done well by me, David, first and last, and I wouldn't lose you for anything.'

So I made up my bed on the floor, and he took the first turn to watch, pistol in hand and sword on knee, three hours by the captain's watch upon the wall. Then he woke me up, and I took my turn of three hours, before the end of which it was broad daylight, and a very quiet morning, with a smooth rolling sea that tossed the ship and a heavy rain that drummed upon the roof.

* * * * *

Alan and I sat down to breakfast about six o'clock. The floor was covered with broken glass and in a mess, which took away my hunger. In all other ways we were in a situation not only agreeable but merry, having pushed out the officers from their own cabin, and having in our cabin all the drink in the ship — both wine and spirits — and all the best part of what was eatable, such as the pickles and the fine sort of bread.

'We shall hear more of them before long,' Alan said. 'Ye may keep a man from the fighting, but never from a bottle of wine.'

We made very good company for each other. Alan, indeed, was very friendly, and taking a knife from the table, he cut me off one of the silver buttons from his coat.

[161]

'Come to my arms!' he cried, and embraced me and kissed me hard on both cheeks

'I had them,' says he, 'from my father, Duncan Stewart, and now give ye one of them to be a keepsake for last night's work. And wherever ye go and show that button, the friends of Alan Breck will come around you.'

He said this as if he had been an emperor and commanded armies; and indeed, much as I admired his courage, I was in danger of smiling at his vanity. In danger, I say, for had I not kept a straight face, I would be afraid to think what a quarrel might have followed.

Presently we heard Mr Riach calling from the deck, asking if he could talk to me.

'The captain,' says he, 'would like to speak with your friend. They might speak at the window.'

[162]

Alan at once held a pistol in his face

I spoke to Alan, and the talk was agreed to.

A little after the captain came (as we agreed) to one of the windows, and stood there in the rain with his arm in a sling, and looking stern and pale and so old that I was sorry for having fired upon him.

Alan at once held a pistol in his face.

'Put that away!' said the captain. 'Have I not given my word, sir? Or do ye seek to insult me?'

'Captain,' says Alan, 'I do not trust your word!'

'Very well, sir,' said the captain. 'But we have other things to speak of,' he continued bitterly. 'Ye've made a great mess of my ship, I haven't enough sailors left to sail her, and my first officer is dead. There is nothing left me, sir, but to put back into the port of Glasgow to get more sailors.'

'No,' replied Alan, 'that's no good. Ye'll just have to set me ashore as we agreed.'

'Ay,' said Hoseason, 'but my first officer is dead. There's none of the rest of us know this coast, sir, and it's one very dangerous to ships.'

'I give ye your choice,' says Alan. 'Set me on dry ground where ye please within thirty miles of my own country—except in a country of the Campbells. If ye want sixty gold coins, earn them.

'It's risky for the ship, sir,' said the captain, 'and for your own lives along with her.'

'Take it or leave it,' said Alan. 'And now, as I hear you're a little short of brandy, I'll offer you an exchange: a bottle of brandy for two buckets of water.'

This was duly agreed to, so that Alan and I could at last wash out the cabin, and the captain and Mr Riach could be happy again in having something good to drink.

*　*　*　*　*

Before we had done cleaning out the cabin, a breeze sprang up from a little to the east of north.

Alan and I sat in the cabin with the doors open on each side (the wind coming from behind the ship), and smoked a pipe or two of the captain's fine tobacco. It was at this time we heard each other's stories, which was important to me as I gained from Alan some knowledge of that wild Highland country on which I was soon to land. In those days it was necessary a man should know what he was doing when he went about the country, when there was much fighting and the people were on various sides.

We smoked a pipe or two of the captain's fine tobacco

It was I that started my story first, by telling him all my misfortune, which he heard with great good nature. Only, when I came to mention that good friend of mine, Mr Campbell the minister, Alan fired up and cried out that he hated all that were of that name.

'Why,' said I, 'he is a man you should be proud to give your hand to.'

'I know nothing I would help a Campbell to,' says he, 'unless it was a leaden bullet. I would hunt all of that name like blackcocks. If I lay dying, I would crawl upon my knees to the window for a shot at one.'

'Why, Alan,' I cried, 'what makes ye hate the Campbells?'

'Well,' says he, 'ye know very well that I am an Appin

[165]

Stewart, and the Campbells have long fought those of my name—ay, and got lands from us by treachery. If they got hands on me, it would be a short shrift for Alan! But I have the King of France's commission in my pocket, which would aye be some protection.'

'I doubt that,' said I.

'I have doubts myself,' said Alan, with a smile.

'And good heaven, man,' cried I, 'you that are a rebel, and a deserter, and a man of the French King's—what tempts ye back into this country? It's a terrible risk.'

'Tut!' says Alan, 'I have been back every year for several years.'

'And what brings ye, man?' cried I.

'Well, ye see, I am homesick for my friends and country,' said he. 'But my real business is with my chief, Ardshiel.'

'I thought they called your chief Appin,' said I.

'Ay, but Ardshiel is the captain of the clan,' said he. 'Ye see, David, Ardshiel is now brought down to live in a French town like a poor and private person. Now, the people of Appin have to pay a rent to King George, but their hearts are loyal to Ardshiel. And from love of him, the poor folk manage to save a second rent for Ardshiel, although it is very difficult for them. Well, David, I'm the man that carries the rent.' And he struck the belt about his body, so that the coins jingled.

'Do they pay both?' cried I.

'Ay, David, both,' says he.

'I call it noble,' I cried.

'Ay,' said he, 'but ye're a gentleman, and that's what does it. Now, if ye were one of the cursed race of Campbell, ye would be furious to hear about it. If ye were the Red Fox . . .' And

I have seen many a grim face, but never a grimmer than Alan's when he had named the Red Fox

at that name his teeth shut together and he ceased speaking. I have seen many a grim face, but never a grimmer than Alan's when he had named the Red Fox.

'And who is the Red Fox?' I asked, still curious.

'Who is he?' cried Alan. 'Well, and I'll tell you that. When our men were beaten at Culloden, and the good cause was defeated, Ardshiel had to flee like a deer upon the mountains—he and his lady and his children. And now in there steps a man, a Campbell, red-headed Colin of Glenure—'

'Is that whom you call the Red Fox?' said I.

'Ay, that's the man,' cried Alan, fiercely. 'In he steps, and gets papers from King George, so that he can collect the rents on the lands of Appin. And at first he says and does nothing

[167]

much, and is very friendly. But by-and-by he found out what I have just told you, how the poor people of Appin, farmers and others, were starving themselves to get a second rent and send it overseas for Ardshiel and his poor children. What was it ye called it when I told ye?'

'I called it noble, Alan,' said I.

'Well, David,' said he, 'since he could not rule the loyal common people by fair means, he swore he would be rid of them by foul. Ardshiel was to starve; that was the thing he aimed at. And since them that fed him in exile would not be stopped—right or wrong, he would drive them out. Therefore he sent for lawyers and papers and soldiers. And the kindly folk of that country must all pack and move, every father's son out of his father's house, and out of the place where he was bred and fed and played when he was a boy. And who are to take their place? King George will get no rent either, but what cares Red Colin? If he can hurt Ardshiel he has his wish. If he can pluck the meat from my chieftain's table, and the little toys out of his children's hands, he will go home singing to Glenure!'

This outburst was interrupted when Hoseason put his head into the cabin door.

'Here,' said he, 'come out and see if ye can guide the ship.'

'Is this one of your tricks?' asked Alan.

'Do I look like tricks?' cries the captain. 'I have other things to think of—my ship's in danger!'

By the worried look on his face, and above all, by the sharp tones in which he spoke of his ship, it was plain to both of us he was telling the truth and so Alan and I, with no great fear of treachery, stepped on deck.

'My ship is in danger!'

The sky was clear; the wind was strong and was bitter cold. It was still daylight and the moon, which was nearly full, shone brightly. Away on one side, a thing like a fountain rose out of the moonlit sea. Immediately after we heard a low sound of roaring.

'What do ye call that?' asked the captain gloomily.

'The sea breaking on a reef,' said Alan. 'And now ye know where it is can ye not avoid it?'

'Ay,' said Hoseason, 'if it were the only one.'

And sure enough, just as he spoke there came a second fountain farther to the south.

And just at the same time the tide caught the ship, and threw the wind out of her sails. She swung round into the wind, and the next moment struck the reef with such a thud as threw us all flat upon the deck. At the sudden sloping of the ship's deck, I was thrown clean over the side into the sea.

I went down and drank my fill, and then came up and got a glimpse of the moon, and then went down again. All the while I was being hurled along, and beaten upon and choked, and then swallowed whole, and the thing was happening so quickly that I was neither sorry nor afraid.

Presently I found I was holding a piece of wood, which helped me somewhat. And then all of a sudden I was in quiet water, and began to come to myself.

I had no skill in swimming, but when I laid hold upon the piece of wood with both arms, and kicked out with both feet, I soon began to find that I was moving. Hard work it was, and very slow, but in about an hour of kicking and splashing I had got well in between the points of a sandy bay surrounded by low hills.

The sea was quite quiet here. There was no sound of any surf. The moon shone clear, and I thought in my heart I had never seen a place so lonely and desolate. But it was dry land, and when at last it grew so shallow that I could leave the piece of wood and wade ashore upon my feet, I cannot tell if I was more tired or more grateful.

*　*　*　*　*

The Ross of Mull, which I had now landed upon, was rugged and trackless, being all bog and brier and big stones. There may be roads for them that know the country well, but for my part I had no better guide than my own nose and no other landmark than a mountain called Ben More.

At last I came upon a house in the bottom of a little hollow

For the rest of the moonlit hours and all the next day, I struggled on, meeting no one by the way. At last I came upon a house in the bottom of a little hollow about five or six at night. It was low and longish, roofed with turf and built of stones, and on a mound in front of it an old gentleman sat smoking his pipe in the sun.

He gave me to understand that my shipmates had got safe ashore, and had eaten in that very house on the day after.

'Was there one,' I asked, 'dressed like a gentleman?'

He said they all wore rough greatcoats, but to be sure, the first of them, the one that came alone, wore breeches and stockings while the rest had sailors' trousers.

'Ah,' said I, 'and did he have a feathered hat?'

[171]

And then the old gentleman clapped his hand to his brow and cried out that I must be the lad with the silver button.

'Why, yes!' said I, in some wonder.

'Well, then,' said the old gentleman, 'I have a word for you; that you are to follow your friend to his country, by Torosay.'

When I had done, he took me by the hand, led me into his hut (it was no better) and presented me to his wife as if she had been the Queen and I a duke.

The good woman set oat-bread before me and cold meat, patting my shoulder and smiling to me all the time, and the old gentleman, (not to be outdone), brewed me a strong drink. All the while I was eating, and after that when I was drinking, I could scarce come to believe in my good fortune. The house, though it was full of smoke from the fire, seemed like a palace.

After eating I had a deep sleep. The good people let me rest and it was noon of the next day before I set off, feeling much better, and much happier for having good food and good news.

Four days of quick walking brought me to Torosay. There is a regular boat from Torosay to the mainland. The skipper of the boat was called Neil Roy Macrob, and since Macrob was one of the names of Alan's clansmen and Alan himself had sent me to that ferry, I was eager to have a talk with him.

Presently I got Neil Roy upon one side and said I made sure he was one of Appin's men.

'I am seeking somebody,' said I; 'and I thought that you will have news of him. Alan Breck Stewart is his name.' And very foolishly, instead of showing him the button, I sought to pass a shilling in his hand.

I showed him the button lying in the hollow of my palm

At this he drew back. 'I am very much affronted,' he said; 'and this is not the way that one gentleman should behave to another at all. The man you ask for is in France, but if he were here,' said he, 'and you had a thousand shillings, I would not tell you.'

I saw I had gone the wrong way to work, and without wasting time saying I was sorry, showed him the button lying in the hollow of my palm.

'I think ye might have begun by showing me that,' said Neil. 'But if ye are the lad with the silver button, all is well, and I have been told to see that ye come safe. But if ye will pardon me to speak plainly,' says he, 'there's a name that

[173]

you should never speak, and that is the name of Alan Breck; and there is a thing that ye would never do, and that is to offer your dirty money to a Highland Gentleman.'

I had some other advice from Neil—to speak with no one by the way, to avoid Campbells and the 'red-soldiers', to leave the road and lie in a bush if I saw any of the latter coming, 'for it would be dangerous to meet with them' and, in brief, to act like a robber.

* * * * *

I crossed over on the ferry and I was set ashore near the wood of Lettermore in Alan's country of Appin.

This was a wood of birches, growing on a steep craggy side of a mountain above the loch. A road ran north and south through the midst of it, by the edge of which there was a spring. I sat down to eat some oat-bread and think about things.

I was troubled by doubts: what I ought to do, why I was going to join myself with an outlaw like Alan, whether I should not be acting more like a man of sense to tramp back to the south country direct and settle my affairs with my uncle. These were the doubts that began to worry me.

As I was so sitting and thinking, a sound of men and horses came to me through the wood and presently, after a turning of the road, I saw four travellers come into view. The first was a great, red-bearded gentleman with a stern red face, who carried his hat in his hand and fanned himself, for he was in a great heat. The second, by his black clothes and white wig, I correctly took to be a lawyer. The third was a servant,

Glenure fell upon the road

and wore some part of his master's clothes in tartan. If I had known more about these things, I would have known the tartan to be of the Argyle (or Campbell) colours.

As for the fourth, who brought up the tail, I had seen men like him before, and knew him at once to be a sheriff's officer.

I had no sooner seen these people coming than I made up my mind (for no reason that I can tell) to go through with my adventure, and when the first came alongside of me, I rose up from the bracken and asked him the way to Appin.

He stopped and looked at me, as I thought, a little oddly and then, turning to the lawyer, 'Mungo,' said he, 'there's many a man would think this a warning. Here am I on my road to Duror on the job you know about, and here is a young lad jumps up out of the bracken, and asks if I am on the way to Appin.'

'Glenure,' said the other, 'this is an ill subject for joking about.'

These two had now drawn close up and were gazing at me, while the two followers had halted a little way behind.

'And what are you seeking in Appin,' said Colin Roy Campbell of Glenure, him they called the 'Red Fox', for he it was that I had stopped.

'A man that lives there,' said I.

He still kept looking at me, as if in doubt.

'Well,' said he at last, 'you are a bold lad, but I don't mind that. If ye had asked me the way on any other day but this, I would have set ye right and bidden ye good luck. But to-day—eh, Mungo?' And he turned again to look at the lawyer.

But just as he turned there came the shot of a gun from higher up the valley, and at the very sound of it Glenure fell upon the road.

'O, I am dead!' he cried, before he really died.

The lawyer said nothing, but his face went as white as the dead man's. The servant broke out into a great noise of crying and weeping, like a child; and I, for my part, stood staring at them in a kind of horror. The sheriff's officer had run back at the first sound of the shot and I guessed that he had gone for help.

At last the lawyer laid out the dead man upon the road, and got to his own feet again with a kind of stagger.

I believe it was his movement that brought me to my sense,

I, like a sheep, followed him

for he had no sooner done so than I began to scramble up the hill, crying out, 'The murderer! the murderer!'

So little time had elapsed, that when I got to the top of the first rise, and could see some part of the open mountain, the murderer was still moving away at no great distance. He was a big man, in a black coat with metal buttons, and carried a long gun.

'Here!' I cried. 'I see him!'

At that the murderer gave a little quick look over his shoulder, and began to run. The next moment he was lost in the trees. Then he came out again on the upper side, where I could see him climbing like a monkey, for that part was again very steep, and then he disappeared over the hill and I saw him no more.

The lawyer and the sheriff's officer were standing just above the road, crying and waving at me to come back, and on their left some soldiers, their guns in their hands, were beginning to come one at a time out of the lower wood.

'Ten pounds if ye catch that lad!' cried the lawyer. 'He's helped the murderer. He was sent here to keep us talking.'

When he said that (which I could hear quite plainly, though it was to the soldiers and not to me that he was crying it) I was immediately very frightened.

The soldiers began to spread out, some of them to run, and others to level their guns and cover me, and still I stood.

'Come in here among the trees,' said a voice close by.

I scarce knew what I was doing, but I obeyed and as I did so I heard the guns bang and the bullets hit the trees.

Just inside the shelter of the trees I found Alan Breck, standing with a fishing rod. He gave me no greeting; indeed it was no time to be polite; only, 'Come,' said he, and set off running along the side of the mountain towards Balachulish; and I, like a sheep, followed him.

Now we ran among the trees, now stooping behind low outcrops upon the mountain side, now crawling among the heather. We ran very swiftly and my heart was beating fast and I could not think or breathe properly. Only I remember seeing with wonder that Alan every now and then would straighten himself to his full height and look back, and every time he did so, there came a great far-away cheering from the soldiers.

Quarter of an hour later, Alan stopped, dropped down flat in the heather, and turned to me.

'Now,' said he, 'it's serious. Do as I do for your life.' And

He rose, went to the edge of the wood, and peered out a little

at the same speed, but now much more carefully, we went back again across the mountain side by the same way that we had come, only perhaps higher, till at last Alan threw himself down in the upper wood of Lettermore, where I had first found him, and lay with his face in the bracken, panting like a dog.

My own side so ached, my head so swam, my tongue so hung out of my mouth with heat and dryness, that I lay beside him like one dead.

*   *   *   *   *

Alan was the first to come round. He rose, went to the edge of the wood, peered out a little, and then returned and sat down.

'Well,' said he, 'we had to run that time, David.'

I said nothing, nor so much as lifted my face. Somebody had murdered the man Alan hated, and here was Alan hiding in the trees and running from the troops, and whether he had done it or only ordered it to be done did not matter. All I knew was that Alan was to blame. I was horrified. I would rather have been lying alone in the rain, than in that warm wood beside a murderer.

'Are ye still tired?' he asked again.

'No,' said I, still with my face in the bracken; 'no, I am not tired now, and I can speak. You and me must part,' I said.

'I will not part from ye, David, without some kind of reason for the same,' said Alan, very seriously. 'If ye have anything against me it's the least thing that ye should do, out of friendship, to let me hear of it.'

'I think that you murdered that man,' cried I, sitting up.

'I will tell you first of all, Mr Balfour of Shaws, as one friend to another,' said Alan, 'that if I were going to kill a gentleman, it would not be in my own country, to bring trouble on my friends. And I would not go without sword and gun, and with a long fishing rod upon my back.'

'Well,' said I, 'that's true! And here I offer to shake hands for I was wrong.'

Whereupon he shook my hand, saying he could forgive me anything. Then he grew very grave, and said we had not much time to throw away. That it would be death to be caught here in a country of Campbells!

'It's still Scotland,' said I.

'You surprise me,' said Alan. 'It is a Campbell that's been killed. If you are caught you will not be treated very well by

[180]

the Campbells who catch you. You will be treated the same way as that man was a while ago at the roadside.'

This frightened me a little, I confess, and would have frightened me more if I had known how nearly right Alan was. I asked him where we should run to, and as he told me 'to the Lowlands,' I was a little better inclined to go with him. Indeed, I was longing to get back and have my revenge on my uncle. Besides, Alan was so sure that I would be treated unfairly here, if caught, that I began to be afraid he might be right. I did not want to die.

'I'll go with you,' said I.

Sometimes we walked, sometimes ran, and as it drew on to morning, walked less and ran more. For all our hurry, day began while we were still far from any shelter. It found us in a great valley, with many rocks about and a fast river.

As dawn broke, then, we were in this horrible place, and I could see Alan was worried.

'This is not a good place for you and me,' he said. 'This is a place they're sure to watch.'

And with that he ran harder than ever down to the waterside, in a part where the river was split in two among some rocks. I kept stumbling as I ran. I had a pain in my side, that almost made me stop, and when at last Alan paused under a great rock that stood there among a number of others, it was none too soon for David Balfour.

A great rock I have said, but by rights it was two rocks leaning together at the top, both very high, and difficult to climb. Even Alan (though you may say he was a wonderful climber) failed twice trying to climb them, and it was only at the third try, and then by standing on my shoulders and

He let down his belt and I climbed up beside him

leaping from there, that he could get up. Once there, he let down his belt, and with the aid of that and some ledges in the rock, I climbed up beside him.

Then I saw why we had come there, for the two rocks, being both somewhat hollow on the top and sloping one to the other, made a kind of dish or saucer, where as many as three or four men might have lain hidden.

All this while Alan had not said a word, and had run and climbed in such a hurry, that I knew he was in great fear of something. Even now we were on the rock he said nothing, and looked very grave. He threw himself down, and keeping only one eye above the edge of our place of shelter, looked in all directions.

Then at last Alan smiled.

'Ay,' said he, 'now we have a chance.'

* * * * *

I think it would be nine in the morning when I was suddenly awakened, and found Alan's hand pressed upon my mouth.

'Wheesht!' he whispered. 'Ye be snoring.'

'Well,' said I, surprised at his anxious and dark face, 'and why not?'

He peered over the edge of the rock and signed to me to do the like.

It was now mid-day, cloudless, and very hot. The valley was as clear as in a picture. About half a mile up the water was a camp of soldiers. A big fire blazed in their midst, at which some were cooking and near by, on the top of a rock about as high as ours, there stood a sentry with the sun sparkling on his gun. All the way down along the riverside were posted other sentries. Higher up the valley where the ground was flatter, there were horse-soldiers, whom we could see in the distance riding to and fro.

I took but one look at them and pulled my head back. It was strange indeed to see this valley, which had been so lonely in the hour of dawn, full of guns and men with red coats and breeches.

'Ye see,' said Alan, 'this was what I was afraid of, Davie, that they would watch the riverside. But if they'll only keep at the bottom of the valley, at night we'll try to get by them.'

As soon as the night had fallen we set forth again, at first with the same caution, but soon with more boldness, standing

The way was difficult

our full height and stepping out at a good pace. The way was very difficult, lying up the steep sides of mountains and along the edges of cliffs.

The moon came out at last and found us still on the road. It showed me many dark heads of mountains and shone far below us on the narrow arm of a sea-loch.

At this sight we both stopped. I was struck with wonder to find myself so high and walking (as it seemed to me) upon the clouds. Alan wanted to make sure of the way.

Seemingly, he was well pleased, and he must certainly have thought we could not be heard by our enemies, for throughout the rest of our night march he passed the time with whistling of many tunes: warlike, merry, sad, dance tunes that made us go faster, tunes of my own south country that made me wish to be home from my adventures, and all these, on the great, dark, lonely mountains, made the time pass quickly.

More than eleven hours of hard travelling without stopping brought us early in the morning to the end of a range of mountains. In front of us there lay a piece of low, flat land, which we must now cross. The sun was not long up, and shone straight in our eyes. It was a little misty, so that (as Alan said) there might have been twenty lots of soldiers there and we would not be able to see them.

We sat down, and had a talk.

'It's like this,' said Alan at last. 'To the south it's all Campbells, and not to be thought of. To the north, well, there's no reason to go north, neither for you, that wants to get to Queensferry, nor yet for me, that wants to get to France. Well, then, we'll strike east.'

'East be it!' said I quite cheerily, but I was thinking to myself, 'Oh, if you would only go one way and let me go another, it would be the best for both of us.'

We went on and began to make our tiring way towards the east.

This was a dreadful time, because of the gloom of the weather and the country. I was never warm, and I was troubled with a very sore throat, such as I never had before. I had a pain in my side which never left me, and when I slept in my wet bed with the rain beating above and the mud below me, I dreamed always of the worst part of my adventures. From my bad dreams I would be woken in the dawn, to sit up in the same puddle where I had slept, and eat cold oatmeal and water, the rain running down my face or dripping down my back in icy trickles, the mist around us like the walls of a gloomy room.

At last the weather changed. The twenty-second day we lay in a heather bush on the hillside in Uam Var, near a herd of deer, the happiest ten hours of sleep in a fine warm sunshine and on very dry ground that I have ever enjoyed. That night we reached Allan Water, and followed this river and coming to the edge of the hills, saw the whole district of Carse of Stirling below, as flat as a pancake, with the town and castle on a hill in the midst of it, and the moon shining on the Links of Forth.

'Now,' said Alan, 'ye're in your own land again. In the morning ye may go and see the agent and find out about your uncle.'

So glad was I that I could only nod.

*　*　*　*　*

The next day it was agreed that Alan should hide himself till sunset, but as soon as it began to grow dark, he should lie in the fields by the roadside near to Newhalls and stay there until he heard me whistling.

I was in Queensferry where the agent lived before the sun rose. It was a well-built town, the houses of good stone, with good roofs. The town hall not so fine, I thought, as that of Peebles, and the street was not so noble, but altogether I felt very ashamed of my ragged clothes.

As the morning went on, and the fires began to be lit and the windows to open and the people to appear out of the houses, I became more and more unhappy. I saw now that

On the hillside in Uam Var, near a herd of deer

I had no way to show that my uncle had stolen my fortune nor to show who I was.

So I went up and down through the street, till I was worn out with these wanderings, and happened to have stopped in front of a very big house. The door opened and a red-faced, kindly man in a wig and spectacles came out. I was so tired and dirty that everyone looked at me twice, and this gentleman was so much surprised with my poor appearance that he came straight up to me and asked me what I wanted.

I told him I was come to Queensferry on business and asked him to show me where the house of Mr Rankeillor was.

'Why,' says he, 'that is his house that I have just come out of, and as it happens, I am that very man.'

[187]

'Then, sir,' said I, 'I have to beg the favour of being allowed to speak to you.'

'I do not know your name,' said he, 'nor yet your face.'

'My name is David Balfour,' said I.

'David Balfour?' he said, in a rather high tone, like one surprised. 'And where have you come from, Mr David Balfour?' he asked, looking me full in the face.

'I have come from a great many strange places, sir,' said I, 'but I think it would be as well to tell you where and how in a more private manner.'

'Yes,' says he, 'that will be the best, no doubt.' And he led me back with him into his house. 'And now,' says he, 'if you have any business, pray be brief, and come swiftly to the point.'

'I have reason to believe that I own the house and fortune of the Shaws.'

He got a paper book out of a drawer and set it before him open.

'Well?' said he.

But I had said all I could and said nothing more.

'Come, come, Mr Balfour,' said he, 'you must go on.' Then I told him my story from the beginning, he listening with his spectacles pushed up and his eyes closed, so that I sometimes feared he was asleep. But not at all! He heard every word (as I found afterward) and without forgetting anything, which surprised me.

'Well, well,' said the lawyer, when I had quite done, 'this is a great story, a great adventure of yours. But, those days are fortunately over, and I think that you are near the end of your troubles. Now let me see what I can tell you. You will be wondering, no doubt, about your father and your uncle?

[188]

He got a paper book out of a drawer and set it before him open

To be sure it is a queer tale, and a difficult one to tell. For,'
said he, 'it all began many years ago when two lads fell in love,
and that with the same lady. Mr Ebenezer, who was the
admired and the spoiled one was, no doubt, mighty certain
that the lady loved him best, and when he found she did not,
he was very angry. Your father, Mr David, was a kind gentleman, but he was weak, very weak. He felt sorry for Ebenezer
and, to make up for his losing the love of the lady, he gave
your uncle his house and the fortune. Your father and mother
lived and died poor folk. You were brought up in poverty.'

'Well, sir,' said I, 'does the fortune belong to my uncle?'

'No, to you,' replied the lawyer. 'It does not matter what
your father agreed to, the fortune belongs to you. But your
uncle will probably say that you are not the real David Balfour,

[189]

Alan strode up to the door and knocked loudly

and it would be hard to prove that he had put you on the ship.
In any case it will probably involve going to court and take
a long time to settle.'

'Well, I have a plan,' said I, and I told Mr Rankeillor what
it was. He listened carefully and agreed that it was a good idea
and that we should try it.

The next night Mr Rankeillor, and a servant of his, Alan
Breck, and myself all met together. Mr Rankeillor knew of
Alan Breck because I had told him, but he pretended not
to know who he was, since, knowing Alan was a friend of mine,
he had agreed not to give him away.

We made for my uncle's house. When we got there Alan
strode up to the door and knocked loudly. For a long time
there was no answer, but at last my uncle came.

'Who's there,' he asked, 'disturbing me at this late hour?'

'It is a matter to do with your nephew, David,' said Alan.

'You'd better come in,' said my uncle, in a frightened voice.

'No, I'd rather talk about it here,' said Alan. 'Either here or nowhere,' he added.

'Well, go on!' said my uncle.

'A ship was wrecked near the Isle of Mull and a lad was found nearly drowned, by some friends of mine. His name is David and he says he is your nephew. My friends have put him in an old ruined castle and will kill him if you don't give me some money.'

'I don't care,' said my uncle.

'Not for your own nephew?' asked Alan with disgust.

'No, I don't care what happens to him,' my uncle repeated.

'Well, perhaps if you won't pay us to let him go, you might pay us to keep him,' threatened Alan.

'Don't let him go,' said my uncle, 'I'll pay you not to let him go. But don't kill him.'

'What did you give Captain Hoseason to carry him off and kill him?' asked Alan.

'It's a lie—I did not do anything of the kind. I paid him twenty pounds to sell the boy in America,' said my uncle.

'Thank you!' said Mr Rankeillor, stepping forward with his servant.

'Good evening, Uncle Ebenezer,' I said, stepping out too.

My uncle looked as if he had seen a dead man.

He was so frightened that, after a talk with Mr Rankeillor, he agreed to give me back a large part of my fortune and I agreed, for he was an old man, that he should keep a small part of it.

Went off down the hill without looking back

The next day I went to see Alan off. He still had his own business to do, and as he was not safe in my part of the country, our ways had to part.

I felt very sad leaving my old friend, and Alan must have been sad too, as we both said very little. At last we had to say farewell.

'Well, goodbye,' said Alan, and held out his left hand.

'Goodbye,' said I and gave it a firm grasp and went off down the hill, without looking back.

Neither one of us looked the other in the face, nor so long as he was in my view did I take one back glance at the friend I was leaving. But as I went on my way to the city, I felt so lost and lonesome, that I could have found it in my heart to sit down, and cry and weep like a baby.